MW01473123

Before I *Forget*

Short Stories from Collective Voices

John Robert Allen
Project Co-Ordinator

authorHOUSE

AuthorHouse™
1663 Liberty Drive
Bloomington, IN 47403
www.authorhouse.com
Phone: 1 (800) 839-8640

© *2019 John Robert Allen. All rights reserved.*

No part of this book may be reproduced, stored in a retrieval system, or transmitted by any means without the written permission of the author.

Published by AuthorHouse 10/25/2019

ISBN: 978-1-7283-3335-9 (sc)
ISBN: 978-1-7283-3334-2 (e)

Library of Congress Control Number: 2019917155

Print information available on the last page.

Any people depicted in stock imagery provided by Getty Images are models, and such images are being used for illustrative purposes only.
Certain stock imagery © Getty Images.

This book is printed on acid-free paper.

Because of the dynamic nature of the Internet, any web addresses or links contained in this book may have changed since publication and may no longer be valid. The views expressed in this work are solely those of the author and do not necessarily reflect the views of the publisher, and the publisher hereby disclaims any responsibility for them.

Contents

Zuzu 1

Harold 4

Barbados – My Island In The Sun 7

Have You Ever Been To Chicago? 13

You Never Know What's Around The Corner 18

Meditative Buddha 22

Waltz Time At Watson's 25

Meet The Other Seven Dwarfs 35

In Sickness And In Health 41

A Graveyard Of The Atlantic 44

High Pockets 48

Tourist Guide 56

Motorcycle Queen: Bessie Stringfield 58

My Story 61

A Lesson Learned 69

A Lift 75

Gustav Mahler On Granger Street 78

The Not So Short Walk 90

An Uninvited Guest 92

Angel Unaware..94

No Ordinary First Lady 115

The "Y".. 118

Wood, Stain, And Electrical Outlets..127

Prime Time 133

The Cupboard... 141

Zuzu

John Robert Allen

While walking on Fall Street in Seneca Falls, New York, you may spot a coffee shop called ZUZU. When entering the shop, you feel as if you are in an upscale metropolitan environment. The décor is done in earth tones of burgundy and brown. Sheer curtains of taupe, burgundy, and cream are casually draped across the windows. Randomly arranged overstuffed chairs and tables invite you to relax and enjoy the surroundings. Music adds to the ambience as you read a newspaper, a book, or work on a laptop computer. The pastries displayed look scrumptious and make a perfect combination with coffee or tea. There is a steady flow of customers, some are sporty looking, some are college students, some are tourists, some are families, and some are the daily customers.

    The contrast between the upscale contemporary atmosphere of ZUZU and the view to the street is extreme. Looking out from the coffee shop, you see old brick buildings from the 1800's. Some of the upper floors are vacant; plywood is covering the windows to prevent deterioration, but underneath there is a historic past. A vacant hotel is across the street, originally called The Gould Hotel. It was named after the famous Gould Pump Company in Seneca Falls. The lobby was decorated with ornate furniture, drapery, and carpets offering comfort to travelers. A fancy restaurant adjoined the lobby. There are plans to restore the hotel to its original grandeur. It will be renamed The Hotel Clarence. Some of the people involved in the Equal Rights Movement that visited Seneca Falls, were perhaps guests at The Gould Hotel.

On July 21, 1923, the First Presbyterian Church of Seneca Falls hosted the National Women's Party's 75th Anniversary Convention. It was there that Alice Paul, a Quaker social worker and founder of the National Women's Party proposed the first Equal Rights Amendment. Years prior to the convention, in the mid 1800's, women were advocating for their personal rights. Amelia Bloomer, known for her outlandish attire, introduced Susan B. Anthony to Elizabeth Cady Stanton on the streets of Seneca Falls. These women continued for years to campaign for equal rights. None of these leading women lived to see the day that women could vote in 1920. Because of this activity, Seneca Falls received the reputation as a "Hot Bed of Women's Rights".

At the street level, flower shops, museums, antique stores, gift shops and restaurants have begun to attract new visitors to the area. There are tours to the Women's Rights Museum, Women's Hall of Fame, Seneca Museum, and other historic places throughout Seneca Falls.

A movie was produced in the late 1940s depicting Seneca Falls as Bedford Falls. It is a classic Christmas movie called *It's A Wonderful Life*. It starred James Stewart, Donna Reed, with Karolyn Grimes who played their youngest daughter. Her name was Zuzu, which is how the coffee shop got its name. Ms. Grimes visits Seneca Falls during the annual Christmas Festival commemorating this movie. She is the only surviving character from the movie. She is often found signing autographs in the ZUZU coffee shop during the festival weekend in December. There was also an angel named Clarence in the movie that was sent down from heaven to earn his wings. The former Gould Hotel is to be named after him, Hotel Clarence.

During my visit to ZUZU, people have come and gone for coffees and desserts. It is much like a metaphor for life- the past is gone-a new life begins-a revival taking place inviting new people to experience the old. There is a modern society looking to recognize women and celebrate diversity. The focus is to reinvent the old and celebrate the new. What a better town in which to do it.

John Robert Allen has been an educator of children and adults for 40 years. He has published five books prior to this latest compilation of short stories by various authors.

Harold

Carole Arkins

I have always loved animals and grew up with either a dog or a cat in residence most of the time. But that changed dramatically during my sophomore year in high school. My friend Marcia and I decided to test Pavlov's theory for our science project and our subject was a full grown albino rat whose name was Harold. We built a two-story structure and taught our eager student to climb little plastic ladders and push through an opening to obtain food. He was very intelligent and learned the ropes quickly. Our Biology teacher, Mrs. Petri, normally took him home on weekends but one Monday morning she said she could no longer do that and asked if one of us could take Harold home for good. I, of course, volunteered, unbeknownst to my parents who were vacationing in Florida.

    My parents returned home a week later and I greeted them with Harold in tow. He was stowed away in the front pocket of my winter coat as I appealed to them to let me have a rat as a pet. Suddenly his white whiskered face and pink eyes poked out of my pocket and Mom and Dad were quite surprised. I can still hear Mom screaming......

After begging and pleading, I convinced them to let our guest stay, temporarily at least.

Our lives were changed by the many adventures of Harold. His cage was in my bedroom but when I was home Harold was allowed to run freely. He was very inquisitive and explored every nook and cranny of the house. We had a record player on which we played 33 1/3 records a lot. One day the music sounded different, like it was being dragged instead of spinning freely.

Much to my surprise there was Harold taking a ride on the record and unable to jump off the moving vinyl!

Another adventure involved alcohol. Dad had left a Manhattan unattended for a short while on the living room coffee table. Apparently, Harold ambled by and decided to take a nip of this newfound liquid. Nothing can quite describe an impaired rat trying to walk down the hall to his cage. An early example of animal abuse, but completely unintentional!

I often wondered how many teachers have heard the excuse, "my dog ate my homework"?

So how about "my rat ate my homework"? It really happened. I showed the evidence to my English teacher and he could not help but chuckle. Huge teeth marks around the edges of the white lined paper and my essay in ink now resembling shredded cheese. At least the teacher was empathetic; no points were deducted when I turned in my assignment late.

Harold lived three years which is typical for a white rat. He almost left us sooner, having chewed through a lamp cord right down to the copper wiring. Sort of a 9 lives type of guy, even though far from the feline variety. Harold endured being dressed up for holidays, going on camping trips in an RV, and the turbulent life of a teenaged girl. He was a great pet and I remember him with love.

Barbados – My Island In The Sun

Renata Reber

For our 25th wedding anniversary, my husband Doug and I afforded ourselves a trip to Barbados. We traveled with our good friends Art and Rita, a couple who emigrated from Germany in the late 1950's, approximately the same time I arrived in this country. We had become very good friends with a similar background and lots in common.

The flight from Rochester to Miami and on to the beautiful island of Barbados was uneventful. Arriving about 11 pm in the darkness, a taxi took us to our beachside hotel room. The clerk opened the door to our room, switched on the light and the first thing I saw was a two inch long cockroach. The critter seemed to be disturbed by our appearance and the sudden light. I freaked out and it was some time for my husband to convince me to better get used to it. Cockroaches call the islands their home.

Next morning all was well when I woke up to a beautiful view of the white beach and the Turquoise Sea. We swam in the sea, laid on the beach, took tours of the island and did the touristy thing, being roped into a presentation for time share opportunities and sales. All sounded well, we were exited and we purchase a time share with "Divi" Hotels. This allowed us an annual two week vacation on the beautiful island of Barbados. As a bonus the Management offered us two extra weeks per year which meant we could spend a total of four weeks per year in heaven. Our friends agreed to do the same thing, only to withdraw from this adventurous opportunity several weeks later. Doug and I decided to keep the deal, it would force us to take a restful and lengthy vacation every year for the next 25 years. We were going to get our monies worth.

Within the first years of our trip to Barbados we became close friends with a couple from Scotland, Angus and Christine and a couple from the UK, Ken and Iris. When we arrived on the island in South Winds lobby, we were greeted by the hotel management with rum punch and of course our friends, the welcoming committee always ready and happy to see us. The six of us started to spend days and evenings together, enjoyed great meals in fabulous restaurant with steal bands playing Reggae music, we visited local shows, danced the evenings away. The Europeans are used to a much more formal evening routine, it was dress up time. No shorts on our dinner table. Dinner began with a "Starter" and the meal lasted several hours. I fell right into it, my European background was not lost. There are no late nights on the island, the evening routine starts about 6 pm, by 11 o'clock most everybody was sound to sleep.

The temperature in Barbados is a very comfortable 82 degrees pretty much year around and it does not cool down at night. The little rain they get is mostly during the night. I like to start my morning routine about 6 AM with a long walk on the beach or through the neighborhoods followed by a long swim in the Olympic size pool. This was my alone time, a happy time. Breakfast was taken in our suite or on the balcony. The routine continued with sun bathing or swimming, sun tanning and/ or burning. In the early years I went to a tourist orientation seminar. The locals told us the "sun bites" between the hours from 11 o'clock in the morning till two in the afternoon. Good time to have lunch followed by a nap in the shade. The six of us booked tours together, flew to other islands and had a marvelous time. I had some trouble understanding the English accent but found it even more difficult understanding the Scottish brogue. When Christine and Angus talked to each other, I needed a translator. They were heavy smokers as most Europeans are, so was Doug. At least most of the smoking was done outdoors.

Several times our adult sons joined us for vacation and we were proud to show off our island in the sun. We had fun on the Jolly Rogers where we jumped from the high rope into the sea, enjoyed ourselves doing the Congo line, singing "feeling hot, hot, hot; No woman, no cry". We hung out at Crane Beach, declared one of the 10 best beaches in the world, the rugged east side, the small fishing villages. The catamarans where always a favorite and so was the local transportation, shabby and very old small VW buses with reggae music blaring. Everybody had to sway in the same direction whether sitting or standing in the bus, otherwise we would not fit. The transportation whatever it might be that day was always filled to capacity. Shopping in Bridge Town, having lunch and visiting the "Colombian Emerald" store were all my favorites. It was so much fun.

We have been doing these wonderful vacations for approximately ten years, never had much interest in trading our location, visiting any place else. We called this our 2nd home.

At one of our evening dinners my husband started choking on his perfectly prepared steak dinner. This was the first time of such an incident, we promised our friends to get this checked out when we are back at home. That was 1993.

We made an appointment with our doctor shortly after we arrived back in Canandaigua. Our family doctor sent us to a specialist in Geneva. After several visits with various doctors, the gruesome diagnosis was esophageal cancer. He needed surgery as soon as possible. We cried together; we had no idea what we were in for. Eleven hours in surgery at FF Thompson hospital in Canandaigua with a one-month hospital stay, then two more months at Strong Memorial with several more surgeries. Our lives never were the same.

The next three years where a learning and life changing experience for both of us. Several more surgeries with lengthy hospital stays followed. 1995, almost two years into the decease, Doug decided one more visit to Barbados. I took lots of specialty foods along for him, we spend most of our time in our suite and on the balcony. Our friends helped out as much as they could. We only stayed two weeks; we knew it was his last time.

April 1996, Christine rang me from Barbados and gave me shocking news. Angus was sitting on a chair waiting for Christine getting ready for a party. She heard a loud noise, Angus felt off the chair and was dead. The coroner was called and he was hauled off to the local morgue in Bridgetown. Massive heart attack was the verdict. Christine had to go and identify the body, she told me she did not have any trouble doing that, he was the only white body there. We laughed over this statement. The hotel and guest were in shock.

May 24th 1996, Doug and I were blessed with new life, our first granddaughter was born. He got to hold and enjoy her for two months. He always wanted a girl. We celebrated Sydney's Christening July 21 with a big party at our house. We invited all of our friends. It was wonderful to enjoy the Christening and the perfect time for friends to enjoy a last visit with Doug.

July 30th 1996 my husband of 37 years passed away at age 62. I was prepared and ready to let him go. How long can anybody suffer? Condolences poured in from family and friends including from Ken and Iris from England and Christine from Scotland.

It was about October the same year; the phone rang from the UK. Iris gave me the terrible news that her husband of 30 years passed away from a massive heart attack.

All three husbands passed the same year. What the Hell happened here? I cannot describe the feeling.

I remembered Iris and Christine with Christmas cards that year. No return card from Christine. After several months I received an answer to my Christmas card from one of Christine's distant relatives (she had no children) informing me Christine passed away from cancer in December 1996.

Schicksal? Mayhem? Now I am in shock.

It was a good time knowing you all. In life we have to move on.

The following spring my youngest son Stuart, his wife Seana and myself traveled to Barbados. We carried a small box with half of Doug's ashes. We went out on a Catamaran. It was stormy weather with heavy rain but we had to do it on this day. It was our last day on the island. At a short distance from shore with Christ Church in sight, we sprinkled Doug's ashes in the sea. His final resting place, a place he loved so much, his happy place.

Barbados continued to be my happy place for many years, till the "Time Share" expired.

Have You Ever Been To Chicago?

Carol Eiffert

It's 7:30 am Thursday United to Chicago. Come with me and my daughter Kris.

I'm sitting next to two non-stop talkers, one a dancer, the other a director. Their talking slows, but always continues… "and so".

We've landed at O'Hare and met with Uber #1.

We're passing a lovely row of townhouses.

We've arrived at our AirBNB, 1264 N. Cleveland Ave., at the corner of Goethe. It is <u>not</u> a townhouse!

And so, we enter a hallway four feet wide, with twenty stairs up, turn left up three, turn left up five, punch in a code, and up ten more steps. Another fifteen-foot hall and we enter a lovely living room and kitchen with city views.

Jim, the owner, had followed with our luggage. We had just enough time to spread them out in our bedroom.

Grandson Adam announced, "Uber will be at the door in two minutes!"

Adam is the grandson who planned this visit to his city of work and play. We are going to meet his work and playmates. And, we are off to his office, the former Quaker Oats Building. Spectacular views of Lake Michigan, and the River Walk.

Uber #3 is at the door, and we're off to Amish Kapoor's "Cloud Gate" in Millennium Park. We gazed in "The Bean" as had thousands of others, before we headed to the Art Institute ... "and so".

Enter the Art Institute and we're walking, walking, walking... up and around Impressionism, down and around Photography, Asian Artifacts, Georgia O'Keefe's "Clouds" as seen from a plane, up and down, hurrying to see it all, up and down hurrying to make our 5:30 dinner at Trattoria # 10... "and so". We walked to a fabulous meal, actually two meals for three, duck confit, (which means cooked in its own fat!).

Without rushing we easily made the walk to the CIBC Theater, where we were thrilled by "Hamilton". It was not a disappointment, and this is where I got the beat.

Before I Forget

As we rolled home in Uber #4 at midnight, the beat continued. I had planned a 7:00 o'clock coffee to keep me awake for the show, it did. At 1:00 o'clock I began to think I miscalculated... the beat goes on, still awake, finally asleep, bingo - wide awake. Finally asleep, then bingo wide awake, could I sleep again? I did, then bingo, awake again.

Whatsup? Street worker in a manhole yelling to a worker above, until 3:00 am. That's allowed in Chicago!

Finally asleep, Friday up at 8:00, downstairs in two minutes. Down ten, turn right, down five, turn right, down three, turn right, down twenty, Uber #5 at the door. The beat goes on.

We're weather-lucky, zero chance of rain, 60 degrees and we're off. Uber #6 was ready to take us to Yolks for breakfast - and it's <u>upstairs</u>!

"And so ..." we just made the 11:00 Architectural Boat Tour, full speed ahead, up the elevator to the boat, ready to leave, chilly, overcast, wrong about the zero chance of rain (It didn't rain too hard, even though we were on top for ninety minutes.)

It was worth every minute. The buildings lining the Chicago River and the twenty-eight miles of shore along Lake Michigan are incredibly diverse, every one a story in itself, another book to read.

Elevator up to Michigan Ave., Uber #7 to the Drake Hotel, <u>more stairs</u>. Grand, with velvet railings, huge bougets, a harpist, High Tea!

"And so…" Uber #8 from the Drake to the University of Chicago campus the Robie House and the 57th Street Bookstore. One hour, one book, "You've Never Been to Chicago" by Neil Steinberg … to the beat, to the beat, Uber #9.

Our BnB awaits, up twenty steps turn, up three turn, up five turn, up ten, punch in the code, collapse on the bed. And so, we are going to dinner with Rochester friends living in Chicago.

It is pouring, but we're Ubering #10 to the Blue Door, a Farm to Table Restaurant in the Old Town.

Down ten turn right, down five turn right, down three turn right, down twenty, Uber #11 at the door.

I am not kidding, the Blue Door had twenty-five stairs to the dining room, not every dining room, just the one we were eating in. The Market Fish (trout) was worth the climb, "and so …" the beat goes on.

Saturday morning, we called for brunch reservations. We were number one hundred twenty-nine at 8:30. We arrived in Uber #12 at 10:30. We were number seven, oh yeah!

Satisfied and ready. we were off the beat. We relaxed into Uber #13 as we rode to the Museum of Science and Industry, arrived at noon. Started at the top floor to see a Boeing 727, stood in a wind tunnel to experience a tornado, and saw a movie on the 1944 capture of a U-Boat. We left at 3:00.

"And so..." tomorrow is our last day in Chicago, and we didn't get to the zoo! It's probably the only free entertainment ... discussion ... we have the whole morning open, plane at 2:00, hmmm, can we get to the zoo?

Two minutes to Uber #14, down ten, down five, down three, down twenty ... to the beat, to the beat.

Wildberries for breakfast, get luggage, then to O'Hare ... to the beat, to the beat, "and so ..." now you can't say you were never in Chicago.

You Never Know What's Around The Corner

Katherine Grey

His name was Sam. He went to the library on Thursdays at exactly 12 noon every week. He went at this time since last month's magazines were put on the "free" table precisely at noon. Every morning Sam would make a little bank transaction such as turning in pennies he had wrapped in exchange for dollar bills. This entitled him to take advantage of the free, aromatic coffee that was left out for customers on the bank's glistening marble counters. On Fridays he walked to the local bakery, the one that marked down their baked goods by 75 percent at 6 p.m. This was his favorite day, as he would buy delicious doughnuts and freeze them. Each morning before he walked to the bank, he would stuff a frozen doughnut into his pocket. By the time he reached the bank for his free coffee it was thawed and ready to be dunked.

Sam had just turned 78. He had bright white hair and the biggest sparkling green eyes. He was what some people would describe as a "poor man." Sam never felt that way though; he would say, "I have enough to get by, and as long as I have my needs met, my church friends, and my faith I am the richest man you'll ever meet."

Sam loved to take advantage of all the freebies he could find. He would tell his friends his little hobby was not a burden; it was a challenge, a "real adventure." He loved to pass his freebie ideas on to his friends so they too could reap the benefits. Sam also helped out at the community soup kitchen for the poor and homeless. He learned about this through his church where he found great joy meeting people from different backgrounds, all with their own story. Sam was never bothered by their tattered clothes or their not-so-pleasant odor. He only saw them as people, people who needed someone to be present, to just sit and listen. Sam always felt when he left the soup kitchen that he'd learned something new, a little story with interesting facts or a life lesson.

Sam was a man who led a full life. He was a happy man. He had been an only child, adopted by parents who were older but very kind and able to give him great love. Sometimes he wondered why he was given up for adoption and questioned if he had any siblings but being so content with his loving parents, he never felt a large void.

Mike was new at volunteering at the library. He didn't really like the idea at all and thought it was a waste of time. It was his daughter's idea. His wife of 50 years recently passed away and he was sad and lonely. He'd been a cranky man before she passed, and he was even more irritable now. He always had a chip on his shoulder, complaining and whining about how life is never fair. Even though he'd found a wonderful woman to marry and share his life with, he never could get over the fact that his mother had put him up for adoption. "How could any mother do that to their child?" he wondered. The thought never left his mind. For years and years, it gnawed at him, and when he focused on it, he became even more grumpy and irritable.

Although Mike was quite wealthy with money inherited from his wife's family, his daughter would not hear of paying someone to go to his house to check in on him. Last month she insisted he move in with her. Her mother, who was a compassionate nurse, always told her, "It doesn't matter how much money we have, family needs to take care of family, that's just what we do." Seeing her dad restless with many empty hours she thought he might benefit from volunteering at the library that was located almost directly across the street from their house. He needed a great deal of persuading but finally agreed so he didn't have to continue to listen to her rant about it.

Today being Mike's first day at the library, he had grudgingly put in his four hours and had only one more item to complete before he could walk home. He was asked to sort through the magazines and put last month's magazines on the freebie table. As he hurried to turn the corner with the heavy magazine cart, he never saw the man with his back to him bending down to tie his shoes. The cart tipped over scattering the magazines on the floor. Annoyed, he mumbled, "Sorry sir, I didn't see you there. You should go to the side of the aisle to do that."

The man tying his shoes quickly turned around with a chuckle and a smile. He began to cheerfully apologize but then stopped in his tracks. The man with the magazine cart had bright white hair identical to his and big sparkling green eyes. It was as if he was looking in a mirror. He knew this had to be his twin!

Together they scrambled to pick up the magazines. Sam searched for words to say to break the ice when he noticed a magazine with the words, "1966 GTO renovation" on the cover. "Now there is something I would have given anything to have done in my life," Sam blurted out.

Mike had also noticed the resemblance between the other man and himself. He felt numb seeing his mirror image talk to him, but a wave of warmth washed over him and his irritability melted away. "It looks like we have a lot to talk about. I always felt a strong void and thought maybe I had family somewhere, and now, just around the corner, I meet what appears to be my identical twin! Take a walk with me across the street and I'll show you my 66 GTO in the garage. I completed its restoration just before I married many years ago. I think we need to get to know one another."

Sam smiled as he bent down to tie his tattered shoes and said, "Well, I see we have a lot in common already." Seeing Mike's shoes at eye level, he noticed they were the same kind as his only in much better condition.

Meditative Buddha

John Robert Allen

On a hot, humid, sunny August day sits Buddha in a rock garden surrounded by magnificently colored vegetation. He is resting in a meditative lotus position. An intriguing facial expression is part of the serene environment in which he sits. The sound of a trickling stream of cool water combined with the geyser-like splash of a fountain in the pond that isolates him from other sounds. A warm breeze makes the vegetation move back and forth creating a peaceful and meditative ambience. A Japanese maple tree, with branches cascading over Buddha, offers shade from the intense summer sun. As Buddha sits in his meditative position pondering his environment, he sees flowers, a pond, a gazing ball, an old armillary astronomical model used to display the principal celestial circles, a birdbath, and birdfeeders. All this is surrounded by the soothing sounds of chirping birds as they feast on the plentiful seeds. Among the vegetation and wildlife are brightly colored Adirondack chairs positioned in a semi-circle toward Buddha.

During meditation, Buddha senses the presence of sensual and calming things. The flowers, of which there are many varieties, have grown to encompass a full spectrum of color. Each plant is unique unto itself just as Buddha is unique. Some flowers are tall and stalky while others could fit into a bushel basket and still overflow with bright yellow or soft pink colors. The pungent sweet air is wafting throughout the garden creating a sense of euphoria. Within the private garden, there is a subtle but sweet fragrance of the tall snapdragons. They are being invaded by bees plunging deep into the throats of each flower trying to extract the rich nectar. Having the nectar and pollen on their bodies, the bees are dizzy with flight as they discover the bee balm plants. There is an intense flurry of bee movement around these plants. Approaching in a swift flying motion toward the rich red flowers come the whirring sounds of hummingbirds. They too are attracted to the nectar and fly at speeds greater than any other birds, as they are darting from flower to flower. Flying slowly with grace and beauty are the Monarch and Viceroy butterflies landing on the butterfly bush that has blossoms of pink tones. Buddha then focuses on the Yesterday, Today, and Tomorrow bush that begins blossoming with a white flower that transitions to purple, then to lavender. The blaze of purple hues is symbolic and a reminder that life is a continuous transition. Buddha then focuses to his right where his sense of smell is heightened by the fresh essence of lavender in the air. Turning upward to the sky, he studies the tall Norwegian pine trees that have survived over a hundred years realizing that they too will endure the long winter ahead. Swaying gracefully in the breeze the smell of pine pitch reminds him of the impending and lonely winter ahead. After a touch of winter sense, Buddha is reminded that cool autumn weather is to come. He focuses on the mum plants at his feet, realizing that autumn is a time of dying down with endings and offering time for reflection of the past. The hardy mum is a symbol to him that many good days are still ahead and that the strong can and will survive. Fall, with all its blazing color and beauty, sets a stage for yet another meditative time. While Buddha continues meditating his stomach begins to growl. Without moving, he senses another aspect of the secret garden. His mouth waters as the herbs create an aroma of culinary excitement. He is bombarded with rosemary, dill, sage, chives, and basil reminding him how much the earth gives in the way of pleasure and nourishment.

As Buddha looks from side to side and upward to the trees, clouds, birds in flight, and the sky, he finds a deep appreciation for the experiences and pleasure of this day. Finding contentment and peace, he is calm and rests in the feeling of comfort and joy. He has only a short time left in this day and life for reflection. Soon evening will fall upon him and he will rest peacefully in his fascinating garden.

Waltz Time At Watson's
Gerald (Jed) W. Marsh

I met Mr. Marchand in 1944 when I was a 14-year-old apprentice at Watson's Timber Mill, smack dab in the middle of the city of Chester in England. Watson's Timber Mill was a huge, cavernous workplace, rearing up like a ruined cathedral on its last legs. Inside, way overhead, there was a vertical reach of grimy windows, none of them cleaned since Shakespeare was a whippersnapper. The high windows strained a barely discernible light through their dirt. To admit sufficient illumination, the great sliding doors, constructs of scarred planks and paint-clogged bolts suspended from roller tracks, were always wide open, closed only at night and on Sundays. We were glad of the light; less welcome was the admittance of blasts of cold weather. This is England, so warm weather was never a concern.

The floor of the mill was crammed with workbenches, circular saws, routers, upright sanders, bed planers, cross cut saws and every other device needed to turn wood into something else. Sawdust floated in the air, trod beneath our feet and settled on every flat surface from tiny window ledge to the shoulders of our topcoats hanging from a row of nails driven into a board.

Watson's manufactured a variety of items, many for wartime use. I helped saw, plane, glue and screw devices called Jeep scotches that were wood flats with bumps on top, used to cradle the wheels of a Jeep and prevent it running amok in the belly of a transport plane.

Watson's grounds also bore a small two-story house, built at the end of the 18th century and a few yards from the timber mill. When Watson's purchased the lot, they took over the house that came with it, and as the house was in disrepair, the new owners renovated it to what was deemed a comfortable dwelling in those far off days and rented it to a retired gentleman. His name was Mr. Marchand, and he was 92 at the time I started at Watson's. Mr. Marchand was not a tall man, but he looked as though he were, for he walked with a brisk upright gait, shoulders back, head held high. His hair was iron gray and his face the color of brown eggs.

All my life I have heard the word, "twinkle," as in "Twinkle, twinkle, little star," but ever since those early days at Watson's I think of "twinkle" as synonymous with the old man. He twinkled. His eyes shone and flashed and smiled. He wore an out of style suit, the color of charcoal, with leather bands sewn at the cuff concealing frayed sleeve ends. The suit showed signs of wear, but it was always clean and pressed. His black shoes were highly polished and always trim of heel and sole. His shirts were laundered at a shop on Eastgate street, the collars stiffly starched, and set off by a stringy dark knitted tie. A co-worker told me Mr. Marchand had been married to a Welsh girl, the love of his life, for more than forty years and that she had died 30 years before at the age of sixty. I never talked to him of that, not wanting to stir memories of his loss. As I said, he was 92, which, to give you some perspective, means he was eight years old when the far off American Civil War began.

He was frequently in his small garden, tending his flowers and shrubs with care, tying up this, pruning that, all the while his dog flopped nearby, absorbing a modicum of warmth from the crazy paving path, indulging his master's extravagance. I would leave Watson's at the end of my workday, and nod to Mr. Marchand as I passed. One day he said, "Hello," and I stopped and leaned over his fence and I asked him what make his dog was. It turned out to be a mongrel. We chatted a bit about his yard, and after that I would stop from time to time and we would talk. Not frequently, really, because there were evenings when he was not there, or I had to get home early, or it was too cold to linger, but often enough that we became - I suppose unlikely - friends. Leaving after work I would stop, open the gate, and as he sat on a little garden seat he had, I sat on an upturned tub, and he told me about his professional life.

I was 14, and, as was everybody at the mill, I was a Communist. The workmen adored Stalin. I listened to them and leaned left. As an apprentice, I was earning a miserly wage of 17 shillings a week. I didn't care about Stalin, but the idea that under Communism money would be taken away from rich people and given to me, was appealing. Mr. Marchand by contrast, was a Royalist. He loved the royal family and the horsey set of lords and ladies and grand houses, and the semi-feudal order that went along with their stratospheric lives. We Commies at the mill scoffed privately at their lordships and secretly referred to them as being "all teeth and trousers."

Mr. Marchand was a musician. He had played the violin in orchestras in the Chester area, supplementing his income by teaching lessons in his instrument.

He told me a little of that, but what he really wanted to tell me, and what I was most eager to hear, was of the 19th and 20th century balls at which he played. I never once went into his house. We sat outside, he relaxed in his chair with an old red blanket on the seat, and me on my upturned tub. He painted a picture of the dances for me. These grand affairs were held under the auspices of the Earl of Chester, local landowners and landlords, and wallet-warm captains of industry and politics. Mr. Marchand and the five-piece orchestra to which he belonged provided dance music for these worthies at the Grosvenor Hotel from 1879 until the 1930s, when it was continued by others.

Ah, me. The Grosvenor Hotel.

The Grosvenor Hotel was built in 1865, and before that there was an inn on the site that dated back to the 15th century. The location is just about perfect. It is at Chester's center. Chester is a walking town and much of the main street, Eastgate Street, is closed to everything but foot traffic. Chester is also a walled town; a wall that was built by the Romans, and later maintained by the Normans, encircles the city. The walking path inside the top of the wall is wide enough to permit passage of a Roman horse and chariot, including the knives that projected from the wheels. At one point on the circuit the wall flies over Eastgate Street, embracing an elevated bridge, and atop it is a handsome clock, a gift to the city from Queen Victoria. Stick your head out of the front door of the Grosvenor Hotel and you can look up at the clock.

The River Dee runs through Chester and on its banks is a lovely park with beds of riotous flowers, in the English fashion. Much of the city is a mixture of half-timbered buildings, many from Elizabethan times, surviving and prosperous. These buildings of wood and plaster were later painted black and white by the Victorians. The rest is of original Norman architecture, and some Norman reconstruction. It is a beautiful city and the Grosvenor Hotel is a great stone edifice at its hub, like a block of granite planted there by *Feng Shui*. The grand balls Mr. Marchand described to me were held in the ballroom on the ground floor at the front of the building, overlooking Eastgate Street, and they continued at least into the 1940s, even though WW2 had visited us. If you remember the TV show The Great British Bake Off, one of the judges, Paul Hollywood, was the premier chef at the Grosvenor for several years.

The rough stone face of the hotel, lighted by the warmth of its windows, is set back from the street. If you face the Grosvenor, there is a revolving entrance door to your right, and to your left and directly above the street level wall of the building are colorful windows in warm and comforting fenestration. The street side lower façade is beveled to the rear at a point two feet off the ground.

I know this because as a determined eight-year-old boy I found that the rough sloping ledge was sufficient to obtain a purchase upon the ledge with both feet sideways and in the same aggressive movement, grasp the windowsill in my hands, raise up and look inside the ballroom. The exercise was hard on hands and feet, and afforded only a fleeting glimpse inside, but it was enough. For a none-too-clean raggedy-ass kid that lived in a subsidized council house, it was a glimpse into another world. I saw handsomely dressed men and exquisitely gowned women dancing. Round and round they went. I could not hear the music through the windows, but I could imagine it. I was entranced by what I was seeing. I did not know Mr. Marchand at that time, nor did I until much later, when I was old enough to work at Watson's.

He told me of the dancers of his years. They were dressed up for the occasion, the men in formal or military clothing, the women in dresses of pastel, cut in the three Fs of the style of the day, Feathered, Floor length and Flat chested. The women wore a flower at one shoulder, and when dancing picked up their skirts an inch or two with one outstretched hand. In dance-speak, it was The Romantic Era. What could be more romantic than the waltz? Mr. Marchand told me the waltz dance sprang from the outskirts of Vienna and was created for the Viennese royal court. You have seen versions of traditional court dances in movies, everybody stiff backed and upright, never touching a partner, all very distant and proper. The introduction of a dance where the couple were in close touching proximity was considered scandalous, which, not surprisingly, helped account for its popularity. It provided a great excuse to get your hands on someone you thought attractive. But it wasn't just that. The music really lit up the dance, and the flames were fanned by the composing talents of Johann Strauss and Joseph Lanner.

Mr. Marchand had a high regard for the gentry, but it was not exactly a two-way street. The upper classes, I learned, did not care for the difficulties of the lower classes. Lady Patrick Campbell, when asked about the large families of the poor and what steps could be taken to restrain their amorous tendencies, replied, "I don't care what the poor people do, so long as they don't do it in the street and frighten the horses."

Mr. Marchand loved the waltz. He thought it the perfect dance music. He was the first to tell me that Richard Strauss's opera "Der Rosenkavalier," was strung together by waltzes. He hummed a few bars of one.

On one occasion he was telling me about the waltz when his eyes lit up, and he went inside to emerge almost immediately with a violin in his hands. He played a few strains from different waltzes. He taught me that the waltz is played in ¾ time, meaning that there is one down beat, followed by two progressively ascending up beats. "ONE, two, three, ONE, two, three." On a mild afternoon, the old man played for a rapturous audience of me, his skilled hands bent around his instrument. He counted off the ¾ time aloud, "ONE, two, three, ONE, two, three." A great deal of my love of music sprang from those little sessions with Mr. Marchand.

The time came when I left Watson's to join the Royal Air Force. Saying goodbye to my workmates and to Mr. Marchand was not easy. But I was 17. It was time to move on.

After six weeks of RAF boot camp I went home to learn that Mr. Marchand had died peacefully in his sleep in his own bed. I was greatly saddened. I reflected on the life he had lived. As with us all, his life had its ups and downs, but he talked in positive terms, and I had no reason to doubt his enthusiasm for life. He was rightly proud of his career in music, and of the pleasure he had given to so many through his playing. He treasured his memories, he shared them with me, and I was glad to listen to him.

⸻

Thirty-seven years later, in 1983, much had changed. I now lived in America with Eileen and our children. Because of my employment in the travel business I had visited London often over the years, sometimes coupled with travel to Europe, sometimes not. In 1983 I had enough free time to take the train to Chester and spend four nights there. I had not seen Chester in all those years. I walked down Queen Street and made a right into the alley that led to Watson's. It was empty, derelict, barred and shut. I was cheered to find that the former secretary at Watson's, Miss Bolton, now occupied the old Marchand house. She noticed me in the alley because visitors were rare. We embraced, and she invited me in for tea and a good natter. OK, chat. I departed with a hug and spent the rest of the day exploring houses I had lived in and places I used to frequent.

It was a strange, disturbing day. Thomas Wolfe was right; you can't go home again. I felt empty. Watson's was gone; almost everybody I ever knew as a child was no longer in Chester. I was glad to get back to the warmth and hospitality of my hotel. The Grosvenor Hotel.

My circumstances had improved since I last saw the Grosvenor, and I was now inside, not outside. I had a charming room. I showered and changed into fresh linen and went downstairs. Here I learned that the bar opened at five, and dinner started in the restaurant at six. I secured a Vodka Gimlet and walked the few steps to the dining room. By this time, my mood had greatly improved. I was happy to be where I was. Beige curtains in the dining room doors precluded a view inside. I turned the antique door knob and walked in. I was quite alone.

The old ballroom had been converted into this dining room. It was dimly lit. At one side was a raised area that had not endured remodeling, and I remembered it was where the band had played. Snowy cloths on round tables bore fresh cutlery, napkins, glasses and flower vases, dinner settings as a result of post-lunchtime endeavor. The tablecloth's floor length white rounds folded gracefully down, and I had a momentary vision of circular pleated dresses extending to the ground. Round and round they went, swirling in a dance, round and round. I imagined the music and laughter.

I walked to the stone-mullioned windows and looked out. Eastgate street was empty and almost dark. I watched it for a moment, and then I looked at the thick window glass. Perhaps I thought to see the face of my raggedy-ass child self, my feet scrabbling at the wall, peering and craning for a glimpse inside the ballroom. I thought about my childhood. I remembered Mr. Marchand with his twinkling eyes and his voice, and what he had told me of another time and its dancers and its music and its charm and its elegance.

I was still alone in the room. After a few moments I looked over the white gowned tables and faced the former bandstand. I raised my gimlet and I said quietly, "Here's to you, Mr. Marchand. Thank you." And I drank from my glass.

ONE, two, three, ONE, two, three.

Meet The Other Seven Dwarfs

By Julie Cummins

Once there were seven dwarfs who became famous. What folks don't know is that there were seven other dwarfs who didn't!

Cast

Scribble – the only one who can write or print
Scruffy – always looks like a rag-a-muffin
Slim and Stout – twins who always stick together through thick and thin
Squeaky – his shoes squeak and he always grumbles
Smiley – always grinning and giggling
Bossy – thinks he's in charge

"Why do 'they' get to be the ones in the famous story," asked Bossy. "We're just as clever and cute as they are!"

He was referring to their dwarf cousins: Sleepy, Sneezy, Grumpy, Happy, Dopey, Bashful, and Doc of the famous fairy tale and movie.

"Yeah," grumbled Scruffy, "'They' get to hide Snow White in their cottage and while they're off to work, she cleans it up. Hi Ho, my foot. We dig in the forest too but all we get is muddy because they've already dug up all the good spots."

"Hey, I know!" said Slim, "What if we find our own princess!"

"Hey," echoed Stout, "Not a bad idea."

Smiley jumped in, "After all, they didn't do such a great job of protecting Snow White, I bet we can do better."

"But first, we have to find a princess," said Bossy, "How we can find one?"

Scribble spoke up, "We could put an ad in *The Forest News* but that takes gold coins. Maybe we could just tack up wanted posters on the trees. I can start writing some up right now."

"Yeah, we could sure use someone to clean up this place," said Scruffy, looking at the messy, muddy cottage.

The other dwarfs sat on the benches and watched Scribble as he printed:

WANTED!
PRINCESS 2 STAR IN STORY
NO EXPERIENCE NEEDED!

The next morning as the dwarfs tramped their way into the forest, Smiley tacked up the wanted signs. "That should do the trick," he beamed.

"I wouldn't count on it," mumbled Squeaky. "I have a bad feeling."

"Look on the bright side, "said Smiley, with visions of pretty princesses dancing in his head, "maybe we'll be really lucky."

"Yeah," answered Squeaky, "we have luck, all of it bad."

The dwarfs plodded off to work and returned home hoping to find a line-up of pretty lasses waiting to audition. But there wasn't even a footprint. Moping, they went inside their messy cottage, ate cold cereal, and went to bed—very unhappy.

The next morning the dwarfs were awakened by a loud pounding at the door. Bossy staggered out of bed and opened the door. Even in the dim light of dawn, he could see that the woman standing in front of him had warts, a big nose, freckles, and a snaggle tooth—a hag!

"I hear from the forest apple vine that you're looking for a "looker" to star in a story," she announced, "and I'm your gal!" With that she pulled out a well-used handkerchief and dabbed at her nose. "They call me Lady Snivel; the lady part is honorary, I dubbed myself."

Bossy turned to look at the other dwarfs, who were still rubbing the sleep out of their eyes. Slim and Stout looked at each other and shrugged their shoulders; Smiley nodded his head and giggled; Squeaky hopped from one foot to the other; Scruffy sniffed and gave a toes up; Scribble traced an OK with his shoe in the dirt on the floor. Bossy took their signs as a *Yes*.

"Phew," he sighed, "you're not what we had in mind, but with a little make-over I guess you'll do. You can cook and clean, can't you?"

Lady Snivel shrugged. "My cleaning's kinda spit and polish, more spit – less polish, but I brung my own sack of apples that I picked up off the ground."

"It's a deal," said Bossy, "first—make-up!"

The dwarfs immediately went to work. Lady Snivel sat on a stool while they tinged her lips with berry juice, plaited her stringy hair into two pigtails, pinched her cheeks until they were apple red, used tree bark balm to cover her freckles, used the ink that Scribble made from the dwarf elder plant to darken her eyelashes, cleaned her dirty fingernails with pine needles, wove daisies into a circle for a crown for her head, and fastened an acorn necklace around her neck.

Next, the dwarfs needed a resting place for the Lady to lie down. They cut down weeping willow branches and wove a hammock that they lined with moss but getting it hung was another matter. Slim stood on Stout's shoulders and Scruffy stood on Slim's as they reached up to hammer the hammock in between two trees.

When Lady Snivel lay down in it, her weight sank the hammock plunk down onto the ground. Another dwarf, another try, as Scribble jumped on. Still not tall enough, so Squeaky scrambled up the dwarf ladder and the third time worked. They placed a nosegay of wildflowers in Lady Snivel's hands and spread fern leaves across her shabby dress. The stage was set.

The dwarfs hid behind trees waiting for the big moment. Hours went by. Just as the sun was setting, a prince came riding by. The dwarfs could barely contain themselves.

The prince dismounted. As he peered at the hag, he thought, "Aha, another princess waiting to be awakened with a kiss!" Just as he leaned over to kiss the hag, a fly landed on Lady Snivel's nose. She sneezed, belched, and coughed, hurling the prince backward with her bad breath as she hacked up an apple seed that smacked the rump of the horse that took off through the woods. "Curses, "yelled the prince as he chased after his horse, "I've been Hagged!"

Lady Snivel sat up, fell out of the hammock, and said, "That was some rotten apple I ate! Horse plops to this, I'm going to try some other story. I've been short-changed!"

As the stunned dwarfs scuffled their way home, Squeaky complained, "Well, that didn't turn out too good. I guess we'll have to do our own cooking and cleaning now."

Bossy grumbled, "Yea, you got that right" as he assigned a chore to each of the dwarfs while he thought out loud.

"Maybe we should try another story and make it our own. Hummm, we could do Beauty *and the Seven Dwarfs* or *Goldilocks and the Seven Dwarfs*. There's a dwarf in *Rumpelstiltskin*, think what could happen with seven? Maybe we could use our dwarf ladder to rescue *Rapunzel*?

"Scribble, get out your pen and ink and start writing We need another princess!"

In Sickness And In Health

Virginia Saur

There is a man who was in wonderful shape
But enemy "ill health," he could not escape.

A heart attack brewed on a cold winter's day,
The ambulance rushing, he was on his way.

The doctors did tests and kept working their magic,
How did we know that the future would be tragic?

Home a few days, he suddenly fell!
911 was called, a stroke I did tell.

Time was so vital, by ambulance he went,
Doctors, and nurses, and tubes and a vent.

The doctors did ponder, a clot or a bleed?
This is the info that doctors would need.

So off he went to the MRI room

the unit broke and then came gloom.

No one could say if it was a clot or a bleed?
So, what happens now and what does he need?

Three long weeks in ICU,
A DNR is all we could do?

Dark winter nights and snow that blew,
Sleepless nights is all we knew.

Many more days of highs and lows,
Things improved, although real slow.

After he moved to the hospital floor,
Improvements continued a little more.

Weeks went by and stress was less.
Hard on family, I must confess.

Then came April and rehab began,
Going home was in the plan.

The end of April the joyous day came,
Would the family's life still be the same?

A move was in order, but where should we go?
All these thoughts we just didn't know.

Before I Forget

A home was found; the packing done,
The move went well in the shining sun.

Our faith and prayers were answered here,
Our lives so precious and oh so dear.

Enjoy each day, be quick to forgive,
You only have one life to live.

This is a story I hoped not to tell,
But Life goes on and all is well.

A Graveyard Of The Atlantic

Richard Booth

In what seems eons ago, we were fortunate to have the famous "Graveyard of the Atlantic" as our backyard. And although not unlike most lighthouses depicted on calendars, we were fortunate the have the Cape Hatteras Lighthouse as one of the first things we saw on a daily basis. Even with the thousands of tourists visiting each year, we unfortunately took the scene for granted most of the time, even with the numerous times we climbed it. Before I relate one of my experiences on Cape Hatteras, I thought it best to explain how this area came to be called the Graveyard.

Cape Hatteras is part of the Outer Banks of North Carolina. There is a long line of small towns that run from Manteo 50 miles to the north, across Oregon Inlet, down to Buxton, the home of the Lighthouse, then going southwest to the Village of Hatteras, a fabulous fishing Village.

The Labrador Current from the north has its path right outside the small part of the island that juts into the Atlantic. From the south comes the Gulf Stream. Their constant collision formed the Diamond

Shoals that went out into the ocean. From the first recorded sinking in about 1560, there have been approximately 2000 ships that had their demise in this part of the world.

Among them were the HMS Bounty and the USS Monitor. Needless to say, the surf can get pretty rough and dangerous a good part of the year. Surf fishing was fabulous and swimming a challenge and sport to many that like the excitement. For most visitors it was much safer to stay near the shore and taunt the crabs and seagulls.

At the time I was there in the mid 50's, there was a small Naval Facility between Buxton, where we lived, and the lighthouse. It was a small 110 person base responsible for underwater electronic surveillance. It was a very interesting job and we enjoyed the sun and sand and excursions to the mainland for our monthly food shopping trips. At that time there was no bridge across Oregon Inlet but an hourly ferry when the weather permitted. In bad weather, this could be a serious problem. Being somewhat secluded, most of the entertainment was held on the base. We had a movie hall (outside) and of course, plenty of libation, mostly beer, affordable to all. We had many good friends and spontaneous picnics and even had to stay with friends when a hurricane hit and we couldn't get fuel to our homes.

So, you can see that in a close environment everyone knows everyone and it is one big happy (usually) family. One of the big concerns was that there were many fun-loving singles, and married ones as well, that couldn't resist an evening swim, so we were constantly trying to keep track of the beer laden men that couldn't resist an evening dip in the ocean, regardless of how rough and noisy it can be.

We also had a small watch barracks the was manned 24 hours for security purposes. There was a couple of bunks, a small kitchen, a desk and necessary facilities. We shared duty assignments and the office was always manned. Duty time at the office was at least once a month. It was a good time to catch up on reading or sleeping. It was required that at least two seamen would be on duty to insure that at least one was awake at all times.

On one particular evening, my shift partner Mike was walking the grounds and I was taking advantage of getting a good sleep. During the night, Mike and someone else came in and were putting one of the what I supposed was a beer drinking casualty in the opposite bed. He then got some coffee and went back outside. I wondered who was the person he brought in and tried to get his attention. When it got close to morning, I called to him, told him who I was and asked if he would like some coffee. I figured he had really tied one on as he was totally unresponsive.

I can assure you he was a solid sleeper as I never heard a peep out of him.

Around daybreak the door opened and hospital medics and a stretcher came in and they put my unnamed bunkmate on the stretcher to take him out. I was getting a little upset at not being informed at this point and demanded to know what was going on. One of the medics said they hadn't wanted to disturb me, but they could not take

"Charlie" to the mainland until morning. I was finally informed why my roommate was so quiet; he had drowned around midnight trying to tackle the relentless surf after an evening of drinking. His body had washed ashore. And the Graveyard of the Atlantic had claimed another victim. Well named.

High Pockets

Barbara Kutner

It was the start of my eighth-grade year in junior high school and my friends and I were excited to be back at school. We were showing off our new school clothes and our "all the rage" saddle shoes as we talked about our summer vacations. We were also very excited because the Future Teachers of America Club was having its fall dance in another month. We were all trying to figure out whom to ask to the dance. The problem for me was that I was self-conscious about being the tallest girl in the class, always in the back row top center for every picture. At dances I was looking down on the tops of boys' heads. It was so embarrassing. I felt like a giant, but one day I couldn't believe my eyes. I was walking to school and realized there was a new boy walking ahead of me and he was TALL!

I learned he just moved here from Kentucky. His name was Herb and he was tall, blond and cute. I heard some girls talking and they said he was in eighth grade, same as I. I was thinking that I needed to meet him. I wondered what it would be like to have a tall boyfriend and how I could approach him? Which boys might be his friends? I learned that he was trying out for the basketball team and my first thought was to hang out by the boys' gym...

A few days later I realized he was walking ahead of me on his way to school. *Maybe I should try to catch up to him. Oh no not today my hair looks awful and I hate the skirt I have on. I'll wait for a day when I am looking my best.*

After school I went home and tried on everything in my closet hoping to find something that he might like. Of course, how could I do that? I didn't even know him let alone know what he likes. *I thought maybe I should take my hair out of the pony tail and let it hang down my back. Boys like girls with long hair, I think. What can I talk to him about? I don't know anything about Kentucky except that they have a lot of horses there and I think my parents watched some kind of a horse race on TV that took place in Kentucky. I can't even talk to him about basketball because I don't know anything about the sport.*

Hmm. I'd better start researching something about horses or Kentucky before I introduce myself to him. I went to the library and learned that Kentucky was quite a horse racing state. They have a race called The Kentucky Derby which is run by Thoroughbred horses on a one and half mile track in front of approximately 10,000 people. Much tradition surrounds the race and ladies get dressed up in fancy dresses and big floppy hats. Everyone drinks a drink called a Mint Julep. I wondered if Herb's family was involved with this in any way? Now at last I have something about which I can talk to him.

Today is the day I introduce myself to Herb. I'm looking really great. I have on a new skirt and sweater and my hair looks unbelievable so here goes. I'm watching for him from the window of my house to see when he passes. Oh, there he is. I'll try to casually saunter out of my house.

"Hi. I'm Barbara Robb. I live here and go to the high school."

"Hi Barbara. I'm Herb Wetzel and we just moved here."

"Where did you used to live?"

"Kentucky," said Herb.

"How come you moved from Kentucky to Ohio?"

"My dad trains horses and worked at Churchill Downs in Kentucky, but the stress was too much for him and he had a heart attack so he needed to find a less stressful place to work. He's working at Thistle Down."

"But that race track is in Cleveland, miles away from here, so why are you living in Fairview Park?"

"My mom says the schools are better here. Well here we are at school. I have English first period."

"I have math. Okay, see you around."

He seems cool. Maybe I can walk to school with him again tomorrow. Sure enough, the next day I just happened to be coming out of my house as he walked by,

"Hi Herb. Looks like we meet again."

"HI." replies Herb. "Do you play any sports?

"I play soccer and baseball, but I'm not very good at either one.

All of my friends play so I like to play with them. What about you, do you play sports?"

"No, I never had a chance. I was always horseback riding or helping my dad around the stables. I started riding when I was four years old, but I think I would like to play basketball."

"You must be very good at riding."

"I've won a couple of competitions for my age group."

"Awesome! But where do you ride now?"

"There is a stable in Metropolitan Park where I ride on Saturdays. I wish I could ride more often but that's the best my folks can do to get me there."

"Hmm. Can anybody go there and ride? Is it hard to ride a horse? I've never been on one."

"Well there are a couple of tricks to it but after you learn them, it's easy."

"The horses are really big aren't they?"

"They weigh about 2200 pounds."

"Wow! That's a lot. Did you ever fall off of one?"

"Sure. People fall off all of the time."

"Do they get hurt, did you?"

"Not really. Well see you later."

I'm thinking maybe I should go the stable on Saturday because I might just run into Herb and maybe he could show me how to ride a horse. Oh dear! What do I wear to ride a horse? It's kind of hot out but I guess I better just wear jeans. Is it really worth all of this trouble just to get Herb interested in me and what if I make a fool of myself?

I am so nervous. My mom just dropped me off at he stable.

I found the instructor, a big burly, no nonsense kind of a woman and after several questions she decided which horse I should ride, a BIG black mare called Beauty. The instructor held the rein and told me to stand on the mounting block and swing my right leg over the back of the horse. Here goes.

Thank goodness she was there because I almost went right over the other side of the horse and would have landed on the ground. I guess I swung my right leg too far over. I can't do this. Herb is not here so I'm going to hide behind the barn until my mother comes to pick me up. I somehow got off of the horse, told the instructor I wasn't feeling well and went and hid until my mom came. I didn't tell her I didn't participate.

As Saturday rolled around again, I talked myself into trying one more time. This week Herb was there. The instructor told us to mount our horses which I did without nearly going over the horse and off of the other side. I felt pretty good that I was able to do that even though I was scared to death. The lesson for today was to walk the horse around the corral and learn how to stop, start and turn the horse. Let the horse know you are in charge the instructor emphasized. That was not easy to do when I was scared, but I did my best. It rained all Friday night so the corral was pretty muddy and full of big puddles. I went around the circle once, then twice with pretty good success.

The third trip around the horse slipped in the mud and rolled on its side with me on his back. When they got me up from the fall, I was covered with mud all over one side of me. I even had mud in my mouth. I cleaned myself up as best I could because I knew my mom would be very unhappy with me if I got mud all over her car. I waited for her to come and pick me up.

"Tough luck." said Herb as he came over to where I was standing waiting for my mom. " You were doing very well. You're a natural. Soon you'll be riding all of the trails without a problem."

"You really think so?"

"Sure. Horses fall in the mud all of the time."

My mom pulled up and I got in. After explaining to her what happened, she questioned me about being sure this boy, High Pockets was worth all of the energy I was expending trying to start this relationship. *As we drove away, I found myself thinking about my mom's question. He is cute. I think he likes me a little bit and above all I need to remind myself that he is tall. No wonder my mom calls him High pockets. I'll try one more time.*

The third Saturday I was back at the stable again trying to learn how to ride that darn horse and above all trying to get Herb interested in me. *I hope today goes better than last week.* Herb greeted me and shared the news that today we were going to ride on a trail. He told me that was where he usually rides but because our class is so large, he has been helping our instructor. He is happy to be able to ride outside of the corral. You are going to love it he tells me. *Oh dear, my stomach is turning to Jell-O.*

The instructor rounded us up and got us in a line to go down the trail. She had very specific instructions about what we should and should not do as we rode. She stressed that it is very important that our horses know we are in charge. *Oh my gosh.* Otherwise the horse might stop and eat leaves or decide to walk back to the stable. She also reminded us if we were at the edge of the trail not to give the horse the signal to back up or we might go right over the cliff backward. She couldn't stress enough that when we were crossing the stream, we were to keep kicking our horses because some of them love to roll around in the water to cool off. Remember, she reminded us again as we started out, you need to be in charge. *I'm so nervous I think I am going to be sick.*

I passed Herb on my way to the trail and he tipped his black cowboy hat which made him look like a real cowboy. *I think he really likes me. I'm glad I came back today. I think today will be the day that I ask him to the dance. This has all been worth it even though I'm still pretty scared.* Again, the teacher reminded us to let the horses know we were are in charge and to remember to kick the horses when we crossed the river.

I was kicking my horse fiercely but I remember hearing the instructor calling out to me, "Harder, Barbara. Kick that horse harder!"

I FELT LIKE I WAS SLOWLY GOING DOWN. YEP, I

DEFINETLY WAS TOUCHING WATER, MY MOCCASINS WERE FLOATNG DOWN THE RIVER. THE HORSE SHOOK ME OFF OF HIS BACK AND I WAS LYING IN THE WATER SOAKING WET. No one was worried about me because they were all chasing my horse. I dragged myself out of the river totally humiliated. Okay, I decided this is the end. If I don't have a tall date for the Future Teachers of America's fall dance then so be it. I declared to myself that no boy, even if he is tall, was worth the kind of effort I was putting into this situation. When I got in the car my mom once again had a comment, "Well, you really did a sopping job of impressing High Pockets today."

After that humiliating experience, I made sure I walked to school on a different street and at a different time. I never asked him to the dance, but my life turned out alright for me because I married a man who was 6'4" tall and who didn't ride horses.

In my career I was a teacher which was what I always wanted to be and then for thirty some years I worked as an administrator in three different private school settings. I like to read, hook rugs, decorate my home and spend time with my family and friends. This is a true story.

Tourist Guide

Leta Mueller

Tourist Guide (excerpts) . . .. The natives are generally friendly, but can become hostile in certain situations. Of particular note: you may see objects closely resembling our (untranslatable), but DO NOT attack them or try to eat any of them, whether you find them stretched out across a plot of grass, or curled up in a resting position. They are inanimate objects, and indigestible to us. Furthermore, they are of value to the natives, who will require you to cut short your visit should you pounce on one and begin to chew on it. We have hopes that our ambassador may be able to persuade the inhabitants to use some other method to accomplish what is done by those objects, but so far, the natives seem reluctant to change their ways, even for the sake of the profitable trade we tourists bring them. The best advice we can offer now is to be sure you have eaten a full meal before going on a local tour where these objects may be found, so that you are not tempted by hunger. Tour guides will remind you of this caution before every excursion on which you may see these objects. Tourists' exposure to inanimate objects so closely resembling our food source is a hazard for another reason. The earliest tourists have found on their return home that they have become less cautious when hunting, and have sometimes been in danger until they have regained their alertness and reflex speed. Our food source is quick, and clever, and can be dangerous to those who are not fully prepared, as you well know. On your return home, tour coordinators will again remind you to be extremely careful when hunting, until you no longer think of the "food-like" objects you have seen on the tour. . WARNING added since the previous printing: At seemingly random intervals, individual natives use weapons to kill significant numbers of other natives. (This is in addition to the constant state of warfare among nations.) Usually the individual assaults happen in places where large groups of natives have gathered for some purpose. Tour guides will make every effort to keep you out of situations where danger could be expected, but the random nature of these attacks means we cannot guarantee your safety. Your cloaks will keep you from being seen, but will not protect you from projectiles. The Consent forms and Insurance provisions have been amended to take account of this relatively new danger. Medical resources, as always, are available on your ship for immediate assistance should you be injured in such an attack. Enjoy your trip! (Excerpts from a Visitor's discarded Tour Guide, translated and now on display in the Museum of Early Visits.)

Motorcycle Queen: Bessie Stringfield

Julie Cummins

Bessie Stringfield was a whiz of a rider but an ordinary bicycle was not her speed. When she turned 16, she asked for a motorcycle for her birthday. Her mother's reply was. "Bessie, good girls don't ride motorcycles!" but strong-willed Bessie persisted until her mother gave in. From then on, Bessie was like a whirlwind on two wheels.

Her mother's common sense reflected the times. In 1927 young women rode proper bicycles in modest and suitable dresses. Riding motorcycles was considered to be ill-mannered and even disgraceful. But then Bessie was far from being a typical young woman.

There were so many places she wanted to go; how could she decide? She took the map of the United States from her wall and laid it on the bed. She would flip a coin - literally! She took a penny from her purse, tossed it over her shoulder, and wherever it landed, that became her road trip. Those pennies became her personal GPS as she made eight cross-country trips and traveled to 48 states.

Her trips were always exciting but they weren't without scary encounters. Bessie faced two kinds of prejudice: first, she was a woman in a man's world and second, her skin was black as her parents were bi-racial.

One of her worst experiences happened when a pickup truck of white racist men threatened her and tried to run her off the road. Bessie was shaken but she was a strong and determined young woman who was not about to be kept from riding her motorcycle.

Equally challenging was her dark skin. Finding a place to stay overnight was chancy as many motels discriminated against black people. But Bessie was prepared for those times.

When she couldn't find a black family who would take her in, she rolled up her leather jacket for a pillow, rested her head on the handlebars, and propped her feet on the rear fender.

One time when she was low on fuel, she pulled into a gas station hoping not to be turned away. She was amazed when the owner, a Southern white man who recognized her, was so impressed with her many riding escapades that he refused to allow her to pay for the gas and wished her luck.

To earn some cash, Bessie entered a track race, but dressed as a man knowing that women would not be accepted. She clearly won the race but when she took off her helmet to wave to the crowd and her hair revealed her identity, the organizer refused to give her the prize money. As for the male riders – they applauded her.

Although she rode like a man, Bessie played up her feminine side by doing her hair and makeup every day and dressed in her favorite color, blue, including her helmet and boots. Even the various 27 Harley-Davidsons that she owned had to be blue.

Bessie didn't hesitate to show off her skills. She loved performing in carnivals with one foot on the seat and one on the handlebars. Her most popular and definitely most dangerous act was executed on "The Wall of Death," where she rode sideways and upside down inside a vertical, circular tank to thunderous applause.

Though she was married and divorced six times, Bessie never had children. Instead, she lavished her attention on her two poodles, Sabu and Rodney. She would perch them on her knees with their front paws on the handlebars so it looked like they were driving. They were a crowd pleaser.

Her life-long love was riding her motorcycle and she rode up until the time she died at the age of 82. Sadly, she didn't live to accept the honor of being inducted into the Motorcycle Hall of Fame in 2002 but without a doubt, Bessie Stringfield left her tire tracks on the trail of women's history.

My Story

Laura Jo Smith

I feel compelled to write this story. I do this so another human being does not have to go through what I did. My only regret is that I wish I knew then what I know now. Every human being is a valued member of society whether rich or poor, regardless of sexual identity and regardless of ethnicity or religious preference. Society feels we all should be a cookie cutter mold. I'm a square peg in a round hole. My whole purpose is not to be "woe is me about my life." Instead it's to save someone from going through life feeling inadequate. Looking back I've been blessed with all my life lessons. People have come into my life because of my circumstances. I called them Guardian Angels from God.

I took the difficult road and am a better person because of it. I grew up poor. My mom was a single mother. She raised my brother and myself without any child support, food stamps or government support. She wanted a house and worked long hours being a nursing assistant. I called the hours she worked the graveyard shift, 3:30 p.m. to midnight and midnight to 8 am. I'm not saying getting help isn't okay, it just wasn't there back then. They didn't have child health plus, food banks, and the numerous programs available for single moms as they do today. My mother at one time, in an act of desperation applied for help. They told her she made $2 too much, yes I said $2, and my mom said she would never apply again.

When I say we were poor, I am not kidding. My father was never in my life, he never paid support and he actually acknowledged that he never had a daughter. That being said, I grew up feeling left out. Being a single mom in the 60's, 70's and 80's wasn't really socially acceptable to a good portion of our society. We were poor but happy. My aunt Frances and uncle Jack always did fun things with us. They made us feel special, they themselves never had any kids. I had three uncles- Bill, Charlie and Lee. They all treated us special as well as they all never had kids either. I called them my three dads. My aunt Marie always told me to be good and work hard. To be honest and truthful. To have a kind heart. Unfortunately, they all passed on without seeing how their guidance made me successful. Many people said "she's a bastard child". As a child I had to ask what that meant, I asked my uncle Bill or uncle Lee as I didn't know what it meant. I remember a few moments of dead silence and tears streaming down their eyes. They had to walk away and come back. As a child I didn't comprehend the enormity of the situation. Then In 4th grade it happened, I vowed from that moment on to prove everyone wrong! At first, honestly my goals were set to PROVE TO OTHERS, not for me. I finally realized God made me special. The hurt and anguish was a lesson for me as later in life I would go on to help others. Helping others with words of encouragement and anonymous sincere acts of kindness. If I can help anyone feel better about themselves, my job is done here on earth. Someday when I meet Jesus, I will drop and bow to his feet. The sacrifice he's suffered for mankind is enormous and even if I fell in Grace and went astray, he was always there to take me back. I've never looked back and I'm following him to eternity. We all make mistakes and can be forgiven. The goal is to learn from them and get back up and dust yourself off and do it again. Success is failure turned inside out!

I went on to college and achieved an Associates in Human Services, and almost a few credits short of an Associates in Business. I also attended Brockport State. After this I went on and got married. I have two children. I work a part time job at a school and help run the family farm. Right now my life is good, but it's hard work! With farming the weather can make or break a year for you. The farm is very physical work but at the end of the day you sleep well. An honest day's work is good for the soul. I will never be rich in dollars but true friends is. What more can you ask of life in having these true friends. You cannot live your life seeking to please every person on this planet or even those in your life. It is an unrealistic goal and you will never please everyone. LIVE YOUR LIFE FOR YOURSELF!! I am not saying be selfish, but you know YOU and only know what you want to do. I still to this day love to shop for bargains at thrift stores, yard sales and auctions! Maybe a little bit too much, but I have it under control, I think! My aunt Marie would take an old dresser and fix it up so you never would recognize it. In fact, my friends and I complete in a fun way to see who can find the best bargain.

My mom didn't have money but what she gave me was wise words to live by when something happens. She would sit down at the table and talk with me and say "in the end I know life doesn't seem fair sometimes but you need to rise above it" - a hard lesson to take as a child. There's an old saying "cream rises to the top". My mother gave me the loving support I needed but couldn't give us a monetary solution. Because of this I learned survival skills that helped me in this world. On another occasion, a person I won't name, stated that I would be pregnant by the time I was fifteen and would drop out of school. She said this only because there was an absence of my father. My mother graduated high school and didn't have children until she was 19 or 20 I believe. My uncle always told me life is tough, be tougher. Words meant that you can achieve your goals but may have to work twice as hard to overcome obstacles in your life. This makes you grow as a person. I have a plaque on my wall that says "when life gives you lemons, make lemonade". Words to live by.

I am a very emotional person and I wear my heart on my sleeve. I gave up trying to please everyone. I focused on my goals but unfortunately it took till I was 55. My friend Angi would listen for hours and hours as I tried to untangle my life and forge ahead. She gave me real advice. I'm now a work in progress, did I say 'in progress' slowly! My friend Linda who is so wise and smart and doesn't even realize it, has also helped me. Still waters run deep- as the saying goes. As I said before, I'm rich in friends. I mean true friends. Through thick and thin Sally, Angi, Linda, Liz, Wendy, Annie, Betty, Shirley and Sharon are just to name a few. I have made many friends from my farm business and have talked for hours over the years but if you ask me their names, I'm like - I'm not sure, but I couldn't forget all of the interesting conversations. Some of my friends are childhood friends since I was 14 years old! I've made many friends over a period of 28 years. I feel that I would never have met them if God didn't put me on the farm.

As I am growing and learning one of the main growths that I am working on and realizing is that "***I will not let the words or actions of others affect me***". People in general are critical. Be true to yourself. You know your intentions are sincere in true so do not allow what people say to you to bring you down. This will be especially hard when emotions are involved.

You need to live YOUR life, not live for others. You will never please everyone. When something happens, stop, and take a deep breath. Ask yourself "am I sincere". If the answer is yes, keep going. I still fall down at times, but get up and dust myself off and do it again. Tomorrow is a new day. I heard a saying somewhere that said "be the person you want to meet". There is a banner at my job that said "character is doing the right thing when no one's looking". Be sincere.

Unfortunately, some people misunderstand my true and deep sincerity. All I can do is know what my intentions are and keep moving. Sometimes with me, it's one step forward and two steps back. In most life situations there are always positive elements. You need to be in the right frame of mind, when all else fails resort to laughter. Sometimes you can cry over spilt milk, although I must admit, I have a good cry and proceed to move on. I am moving on. I find humor in the most bizarre situations at times. There have been times my friend and I laugh so hard we were crying. if you look hard enough, there is humor in most life situations unless it is of a tragic nature. I am going to set a good example when people look at me. My mother would say to me "walk a mile in someone else's moccasins" because one never knows what they have been through. Heartbreak and pain has no economic boundaries, rich or poor, it still hurts the individual. I'm definitely not perfect, but once words are said they leave an incredible mark on the heart, so think before you speak. Ask yourself 1) is it necessary 2) is it kind and 3) will it do any good. It's so hard to walk away when falsely accused but do your best. Then if you need to vent, which I do, I call my best friend and tell her I need to get something off my chest. A true friend and comfort is a gift from God. I have a key chain that says "she's my best friend, she knows all my secrets"! All kidding aside, I couldn't live without a handful of my best friends. They accept me the way I am, warts and all!!! When I get really frustrated, I will cry in lieu of harsh and unnecessary words. Some may call it a weakness, but to me it's self-preservation. I have not said something that I did not take back! I think that sometimes when people mistreat others in life, you can either retaliate or walk away. You still have the right to be upset if you were wrong and you didn't stop to stoop to their level!!! I have come a long way from being insecure and apologizing for things I didn't do. For a very long time I felt like a doormat personality. However, I am stronger, but at times still weak. It's an ongoing process. I choose laughter, kindness and love. I tend to shy myself away from negative people because life is a gift. You only get one, so start living. Make laughter, love, and positivity fill your day. The good days outweigh the bad ones. Be the change. Of course death, illness and sadness needs its own mourning and healing time. So please don't ever deny yourself of that. Always look for beauty in life. Things could always be worse, surround yourself with good people and your life will improve. While writing this I have re-lived many sad moments and events, but it has been so freeing to let those moments go, forever.

I recently went in April 2018 on a walk to Emmanuel. It let a lot of negative components of my life evaporate into time. Getting closure is so freeing. The negativity is no longer holding me down. To all who have made inappropriate comments towards me, I forgive you. Sometimes one in particular, letting go of very toxic relationships with abusive verbal attacks can be hard. One doesn't realize the scars it leaves on one soul. It has been a hard, tumultuous journey, but I'm really truly on my way to healing.

I have been told several times "when you hold onto things it only hurts your progress", forgive the past and make your future. Although it may at times continue to come up on me once in awhile, the memory is fading. If I have a moment where I bring those memories to the present then I can call on God and my dear close friends to work it through. Honesty and kindness can move mountains. I now wake up every day and say "I can", the words "I'm stupid" or "I can't do that" are no longer a part of me. It's a long journey and I'm blessed the Lord put me on it. I've grown and met wonderful Guardian Angels along the way. People please, verbal abuse and put-downs are very toxic to one's self-esteem. It may be the giver of these comments doesn't care, but if one thing comes out of this, "kindness costs nothing". These comments are like a knife to the heart. If this story is beneficial to one person then it will have served its purpose. In closing "choose kindness, you are beautiful".

A Lesson Learned

Barbara Kutner

The morning sun was streaming through the bank of windows into our nursery school classroom. The window sills were lined with pink geraniums in full bloom creating a place of beauty for the children to enjoy. The room was painted yellow and offered a bright, cheery environment for them to learn and play. We were at the door of the three-year old's classroom, welcoming them to this special place.

Soon there was a steady but purposeful hum in the room. The housekeeping area was occupied by two little girls. Dress up clothes were hanging nearby and the girls were seated at the child sized table and chairs dressed in their finery, large hats and white gloves. They were discussing what they were pretending to be eating. The baby doll was in her cradle being rocked by "the mother." Joey, another student was watching.

Other children were busy in the block area building a road and a garage for their cars, while others were building a house for the toy rubber family they said lived there. Some other teachers were observing the school on this day and the children kept an eye on them.

Soon the children had built an enclosure using large red cardboard brick building blocks to remove the visitors from their view so they could continue their play without being watched. Children are great problem solvers. Joey, for whatever reason, did not join the play.

The art project for the day was painting with a half of a potato into which a heart had been carved. The children dipped the potato into a stamp pad made with paper towels and thick paint enabling them to print with the potato and create a valentine picture. They were wearing, with pride, their father's old shirts which served as paint smocks as they joyfully created their designs. Joey ventured a little closer but did not join in.

Two children in the book corner were having trouble sharing and the teacher skillfully coached them. The children knew they could count on their teacher to help them solve their problems fairly. Again, Joey was a bystander.

It is normal for preschoolers to argue and demand their rights as they seek their independence. We teach them to use words instead of grabbing what they want or sometimes hitting another child. Other preschoolers need help asserting themselves. For three-year old's, it takes time for them to internalize these lessons and we were constantly working with the children to teach them how to appropriately get their needs met.

The children were developing nicely and pretty much as expected except for one little fellow whom you've already met named, Joey. He was small of stature and was the youngest of three children in his family. His hair was brown and cut in a Buster Brown style. Joey was a puzzle to us. He was quiet and could have been easily over looked. He would often just stoop down in one spot and not move. He wouldn't say anything. Just sat that way for a period of time and wouldn't respond to our suggestions to help him. Many times, he'd withdraw to a corner of the room and be by himself. He didn't seem all that unhappy but this was unusual behavior which gave us concern and we wondered if he wasn't well. We discussed this with his mom and she had no explanation for his behavior. A preschool teacher's job is among other things is to observe behavior and try to interpret it. We were stumped and had no idea why he was exhibiting this behavior.

One day he told us that he was tired because his dad was waking him up during the night to practice fire drills and he felt scared there was going to be a fire in the house. The dad, we were sure was well-intentioned but this was too scary a situation for a three-year-old. Joey seemed overly concerned about doing something wrong at school and if he thought he had been "bad" in his little mind he became very anxious. Sometimes he complained of stomach aches. He wouldn't let us touch him. We tried all kinds of ways to help him but he was unreachable. We began to put the pieces together and were concerned that Joey was experiencing some kind of abuse. We were just beginning to hear about this problem for children and were not well informed about how to handle these situations. As preschool teachers we were expected to report this even if it was only a suspicion. We contacted our school consultant, a psychiatric social worker who was on retainer to our school and offered counseling and help to teachers and parents when needed. He suggested we try to talk to the parents before he reported the incident and gave us some suggestions before we approached the parents.

During a parent conference we met with Joey's parents who were college educated bright people who seemed to be at a loss about how to deal with Joey. They shared with us that Joey "did not fit the mold" in his family the way the other two children did. He was always testing the limits causing his parents to become frustrated and they resorted to inappropriate punishment. We talked about making sure the punishment was appropriate to the behavior and that the purpose of the discipline was not to be punitive but be such that Joey learned from his parents the correct behavior and how to achieve it. We also suggested that they work on one behavior at a time. When that behavior had been mastered, we suggested they give Joey high praise and then move on to the next behavior. They appeared receptive to our suggestions and thanked us for our help. We felt the father was definitely in charge in this family and it was he who had unrealistic expectations which caused him to clash with Joey. That said we felt the father genuinely loved his son and that they heard us. So there was no report made.

We kept a close eye on Joey but knew the behavior wouldn't change overnight. We did, however, feel that Joey seemed to be relating to the other children after several months in a bit more relaxed manor which was encouraging to us.

The school year ended and Joey's parents didn't enroll him for his four-year-old year at our school. We heard he was going to a different nursery school in town. Could it be that his parents changed schools because they knew we were suspicious of things happening at home? We knew the school he was attending and were glad he was at one with a fine reputation. We often wondered about this family and were hopeful that things were better for Joey.

Sadly half way through the next school year we received word that Joey had died. His father, in fit of anger, had thrown Joey down the stairs. We couldn't even begin to understand the anger, grief and sorrow his family must have felt. We had a hard time not blaming ourselves.

We were heartbroken but also afraid that we hadn't done our job of reporting our suspicions. The district attorney's office called and made an appointment to talk with us about Joey. We had very carefully documented all of our observations and conversations which again is a large part of a preschool teacher's job, observing and recording children's behavior. A representative from the district attorney's office was sent to our school to question us about our actions and observations. He spent a long time with us and after many questions he left without the intention of taking any action against us. We were very relieved, but full of guilt, wishing we had done more to help Joey.

The father was not charged as the authorities thought living with what the father had done was punishment enough. We were unsure how we felt about this decision and could see both sides of him being convicted or not. It was a topic of conversation among us for quite a long while.

This experience was beyond difficult. Teachers and other persons of authority were just beginning to receive training in identifying abuse and reporting their suspicions. We were not well prepared for dealing with these problems because they were kept hidden for so many years. After this incident we read and took classes to learn everything we could about the forms of abuse and how to identify them. The next time, years later when an incident was brought to our attention, we knew what to do and, thank goodness for the wonderful teacher's notes of the child in question, this case had a happier ending than Joey's. This experience was a lesson learned the hard way, fortunately though it served to help another child in a similar situation. When mistakes are made, the best we can hope for is that we learn from them.

A Lift

Jewel Wink

The fog will lift.
Maybe it will lift my heart!

I hear his voice.
"Good wind, sun. What could be better?"
"Put up the sail, First Mate!"
I put up the sail.

It always made me feel complete…
me being there with Grandpa.
We head toward the bay.
All our cares were left on the dock.

Grandpa loved me without saying it much.
He taught me to sail and I listened to his words.

Once a storm had come up fast.
We were headed for the dock.

We spotted the boys.

They were holding onto the side of their boat.

The waves slapped hard.

Our sail cracked like a whip in the wind.

I had the tiller.

Grandpa got them on board.

Soon the coastguard came.

We got a medal for this from our town.

Grandpa had broken his ribs pulling those boys onto the sailboat.

Grandpa said, "Anyone would have done it."

I keep that medal in my drawer.

These later years I helped him in the boat.

I could see he was in some pain.

He never said.

Being here at the boathouse,

The echo of his voice is strong.

He wanted the best for me.

"You can do anything you set your mind on."

Or…

"Look for the best in people.

You'll always find it."

I pin on our medal on my shirt.

I put Grandpa's ashes in the boat and head toward the bay.

I scatter his ashes.

The fog has lifted…

And so has my heart.

Jewel Wink is a wife, mother, grandmother and great grandmother, retired teacher and educational evaluator, writer for the Canandaigua Wood Library Writers Group and Ontario Yates County Writers for Literacy.

Gustav Mahler On Granger Street

Gary Baldwin

The leaves on the trees were almost gone now, with a few small attached brown hangers-on. The wind and rain had taken them except for the large tree in the backyard which doesn't lose its leaves until at least Thanksgiving. The front lawn on Granger Street, a quiet street needed raking, having been neglected for quite a while. The air was changing, and once again I began my travels through the labyrinth of my studies of Gustav Mahler studies, Austrian composer and conductor that occupied my time since 1970. He has become a friend and counselor over these many years. My computer sits directly to the right of the window that looks out over the street. I am on the second floor and by looking up against the window I can see two houses in both directions. Although there is little reason to suggest that there is any real interest in the comings and goings, people do take walks, with and without their pets, and there is always a number of children scurrying around, establishing a background of small-town normalcy.

It was this sort of day that found me working in my room, as

Before I Forget

I looked out of the window and glimpsed a short, small, thin gray figure. With a large forehead, disheveled hair, and 'Harry Potter' glasses. He also had a most unusual walking gait. His black cape and top hat seemed to have come from a theatre costume shop. He could have wandered away from the Veterans' Hospital up at the end of the street. It certainly has happened before.

He was walking with purpose when I first sighted him. Curious about the gentleman with the black graying hair, I got up and went to the window in the guest room to get a closer look. He had stopped directly across Granger Street looking at what appeared to be the window where I was. I jumped back out of sight, and when I returned to the window there was no sign of the black caped veteran. I ran downstairs out the front door and looked quickly up and down to see him – no signs! He had disappeared or he had never been there at all.

Later that week when I was browsing through my Mahler Library looking at photographs, I came across a very famous picture of Mahler walking with Mengelberg near Amsterdam. The "Lost Veteran's" attire as I had seen it from the window of my study looked remarkably similar to Gustav Mahler's in the photograph.

As the days went by I had convinced myself that there was no relationship between the "Lost Veteran," Gustav Mahler, or the man I had seen. And if I were to suggest such a linkage, I know that it would be perceived as an *illusion and hallucination.* **I left it alone - until Maestro Mahler returned in the spring.**

Months had passed. Winter had come and gone, and the world was looking a little bit brighter. The winter chill was replaced by warmer air in anticipation of returning birds. There had been plenty of time to think about my hallucination and to rationalize its occurrence as nothing but extracurricular mental activity. Seeing Gustav Mahler on Granger Street in the 21st Century could not be supported by anything tangible in my background.

I noticed the "veteran wanderer" in the late morning prior to the noon lunch hour. His movements seemed more direct and focused, as if he was going to a specific destination – on the way to a scheduled appointment on the 'Ringstrasse' or perhaps lunch at the Grinzinger Tavern. Besides the black hat and cape, the man wore a three-piece dark gray suit. It appeared to be wool, or at least it seemed full and heavy. A little heavy for the season. Also, he wore a black bow tie hastily arranged. They were not American made, and his shoes glistened in the warm spring sun.

My position was as before. From the second-floor window in my home I watched intently. The man with his black intense eyes stared directly at me. I was numb! Then I ran! If this was a hallucination, I intended to confront the image as close as I possibly could and perhaps have it dissipate as I approached. Scurrying down the fourteen steps to the front door I realized that I had brought nothing tangible with me to show the man. Nothing that would help me verify to myself that he was either real, an imposter, or a ghost. In my mind I knew of course that when I got there he would be gone. If only I could have brought with me a book of Alma's or Bruno Walter's book. That would have given me evidence.

I turned the corner out of my driveway and out to the street – and in my own thrust ran directly into the gentleman! Neither one of us lost our balance even though I outweigh him significantly. Face to face we stood…the image of Mahler starkly inches away. Not only was I breathless from the run, but I was stupefied at the resemblance. He placed a simple black bound book in my hand. I took it and noticed his long lean fingers – piano hands.

The man said "Thank you for this. I enjoyed it very much. I hope you will write more."

I was stunned. None of this made sense. What was he talking about?

I fainted!

I woke up on the side walk in front of my neighbor's home. It had only been a few minutes ago, I checked my watch to confirm. The gentleman was gone. Would he return?

I waited until I got back up into my second-floor study before I opened the book.

Having opened the book, the title page read <u>Das klagende Lied: The Establishment of the Mahlerian Style.</u> This was a manuscript from my college days. Stunned by the man and the manuscript, and how it even got into his hands, my mind raced with potentialities. I returned to my room and inspected my library to find the place in which the manuscript had been placed. There, in plain sight was the empty space where I gently replaced it back into position- along with other Mahler materials gathered over thirty-five years of research and investigation. What was going on? When would I wake up from this dream? Did someone actually appear to me, but briefly, looking and acting a great deal like the great Austrian composer?

Months must have passed on Granger Street, as well as seasons, and the image of Mahler in my mind was etched like steel and fire against a cloudiness of perception. It was the spring of the following year when the image appeared – making his way up Granger from the east side. His gate was uneven, but strong as always before. I watched as he came closer to the house from where I was watching, not knowing that I had been holding my breath for several seconds. The bright inquisitive eyes caught sight of me. I ran down the stairs, grabbed my red Lands' End's wind breaker, took nothing with me and confronted the figure at the end of the driveway! Or perhaps it would be better to say **I gazed at the figure in awe and terror! What if he wanted me to sing some Wagner?** A hallucination; a ghost; an angel; the devil; schizophrenic or depressive?

He extended his hand out toward me and as we shook hands he said "My name is Gustav Mahler. I left my wife Alma at home. She doesn't think I should be visiting you!"

"Should we walk?" I said.

"He nodded".

I thought for sure that I was going to have a heart attack. I was feverish and my chest was pounding with anxiety. I stepped into his path and we preceded to walk west toward main street and then north to a neighborhood coffee shop. Very small, and thankfully quiet. Nothing was said during this walk. Once in the shop we took a seat at a table. I picked up two coffees. I assumed black for him and cream for me. I didn't want to confuse him with the multiple choices one has in the 21st Century. We can wait for 'Starbucks' on another day. He was looking intensely out the window at the passing traffic. "What do you call these moving vehicles that pass so quickly?"

I responded "Gas propelled vehicles: cars, trucks, buses, all used for the transportation of people and goods.

Looking straight into my eyes, he says "I believe my time has come." He continued in a soft pleading voice, "I have decided to visit and see for myself. Will you be my guide?" He got up and we left the coffee shop. I turned to close the door behind me. Turning back toward Main Street he had disappeared. No sign. I walked home realizing the type of preparation I was going to need to do. Took some aspirin and laid down on the couch. Perhaps I would feel better when I woke up.

I now had some real feelings that he might return, but just when I did not know. I had more feelings that I was going crazy. The hallucinations and dreams were beginning to project a serious negative behavior pattern on my life. Things seemed always in flux as I hastily prepared for his return. I told no one, and tried to maintain my balance of the appearances of GM and the day to day reality of my life. The longer he remained in the dark recesses of my mind, the more I felt comfortable that the pattern would not continue and I would be freed from my obsessive thoughts and anxiety.

It was summer when I saw him again, and this time he never went very far for very long.

He was here to visit and explore his legacy!

Now began a long period of time when Mahler would come and go as we would plan our trips around his performances and musical events that I thought he would be interested in. I tried to spend time with 21st Century music, both orchestral and opera. Some he hated, some he was delighted with. He was particularly fond of Shostakovich, Stravinsky, Adams, Nielsen, and Britten. I shared with him conductors' legacies of Bruno Walter, Stokowski, Otto Klemperer, and Leonard Bernstein. There was simply too much available for him to process - one hundred years of music history which because of the two world wars and now terrorist interventions, had shattered traditions and cultural linkages. There was no musical school either in Europe or in America. Every composer was his own style and banner carrier. I showed him the advantages of technologies as I sat at my computer and logged in live stream music performances from the Berlin Philharmonic Orchestra, The Gothenburg Symphony, as well as opera and recital performances from all over the world. He got really excited and comfortable with the CD media format and its capabilities. I showed him the access capabilities of the computer to find composers' music and to investigate and study them. I took the time to log into the New York Philharmonic Archives and bring up his original score of Symphony No.1 that he conducted in New York, and included his own personal markings! "I wish I had one of these machines!" he exclaimed!

Mahler would not always appear on Granger Street after that. He would often arrive quite unannounced. Many times we would plan our outings as I would work through things that I thought would be of interest to him. Some required advance planning, some did not. One week I was so selfish – went through with him the two seminal scholarly biographies regarding his life and music. La Grange and Mitchell. Of those events that have changed our global society over a period of 100 years, there was the arts revolution to take advantage of. Having no knowledge for how long or for what time he would be around – I had to draw on my own limited experience as one person. He had not made himself known to anyone else, and at any other time, – to my knowledge.

Although he had had the experience of riding in an automobile while he had conducted in New York, it was quite a different experience riding in a late model car down the expressway at 70mph! It was February and the appropriate weather was upon us. As we passed through the cities of Buffalo, Erie, Pennsylvania, - on our way to Cleveland I was anticipating the composer's reaction to the upcoming performance. At that point in time, I had not acquired a score of the performing version of Mahler's 10th Symphony prepared by Derek Cooke. I did find a copy for him before he was to leave.

There was no preparation for the composer for what he was about to hear, other than his completed Adagio. Simon Rattle was conducting this evening. As I settled into my plush velvet green seat, Gustav did his usual tour of discovery. There was no need for a seat for him, since he passed unnoticed throughout the hall – as he was accustomed to do on these occasions. I would often watch him, but not being able to find him until suddenly he would appear in the percussion section looking over equipment and the music on the stands sitting on the stage. Where he actually sat depended on the availability. But generally, he could find an empty seat somewhere, and if not, he didn't mind standing, leaning, or walking around the outer wall of the hall – this in fact often helped his natural nervousness.

Leaving Severance Hall that night, I found him both quite sullen and agitated – switching gears between what he had heard, and how it affected him. He had been extremely moved by the performance, both in its 're-incarnation' and its content. He marveled at the discipline and performance generated by the Cleveland Orchestra and its conductor. He seemed very pleased with his work, and very grateful to Cooke and his compatriots for their commitment to his music.

The review of the concert in the Cleveland Plain Dealer noted during the space of time that the Mahler symphony was being performed, there existed a genuine sense that the "spirit" of Gustav Mahler' was present in the hall. If I had any doubt that the composer was not at my side, this sustained the ballast and belief in the composer's presence.

The trip home seemed quick. The conversation lively. I let him off at the corner of Main Street and Granger at the Coffee Shop always wondering and waiting for his next return. Before I went to bed that night I went to the music room, took the 'Adagio' off the bookshelf and looked at it quickly and returned it to its place. The only other thing he commented on after the performance was that 'The Purgatoire' movement seemed somewhat misplaced within the framework of the symphony. He seemed to have some doubts about it. He moved on quickly to other things.

The flight tickets for Salzburg lay on my bed stand.

Walking across the plaza toward the Dome Cathedral in Salzburg, I suddenly realized that the Maestro was suddenly at my side. He would often show up on the spot without any warning. I think he enjoyed his omnipresent abilities – even though he never showed himself to anyone else but me. "SALZBURG!" he acclaimed. "Where are we going to today?" I pointed to the Dome Cathedral and said "concert – Bruckner I think." The connecting links fell into place with such fluidity that it was impossible to dismiss their connections with the Maestro. Mahler's orchestra the Vienna Philharmonic, in an opening concert performance at the Salzburg Festival – Bruckner's *Te Deum* under its present conductor Herbert von Karajan. After a crushing entrance among the thousands of people getting into the cathedral, we found a place to stand at a huge column on the left side; at the front; only a few feet from the cordoned off area for the orchestra. The polyphonic lines of the *Te Deum* were of course dissolved into the acoustical environment, but the overall effect was colossal and reverent in its reverberation throughout the cathedral arches. The *Te Deum* had special significance to him. He had performed it in Hamburg at a sacred concert for Good Friday 1892. It was a significant success for the conductor and composer. Later, we would find in Mahler's 8th Symphony the echoes of monumentalism that Mahler would recreate from the inspiration of that he drew from the Bruckner. A half hour later, back in the splendid sunshine of the plaza. I pointed out in the sky the passing of a private jet over the city of Salzburg. I said "Karajan," and Mahler quipped "He gets around almost as fast as I do."

And suddenly he was gone! I thought I saw him going around a corner and heading for the Castle, but I could not be sure of any of it happening

Having finished his morning treat of apricot cobbler and several cups of black coffee freshly brewed at Starbucks, he sat back mildly comfortable – not a usual tendency for this great man. His traveling clothes were on. His cape and hat sitting closely by his side. Looking shyly around the screened in porch back at home – he finally spoke.

It is time for me to leave. Alma says that I don't belong to this time. She is right you know. I yearn for my little opera house in Vienna and the solitary walks in the Alps – unfortunately they are no longer a part of this world – your world. My time has come. The music is everywhere and I could never have expected this renaissance of music as I have seen it through our journeys together. The world is different, but I am still here for everyone to share. My time to leave is now, and there will be no reason to return.

He quietly got up, put on his cape and hat, and began his journey down Granger Street. He moved toward the Veteran's Hospital from which I had first thought he had come. It was a fall day much like the one when I first sighted the great man on my street. I watched his awkward, halting step that I had finally managed to walk with – as he disappeared around the corner to Pleasant Street and out of sight.

He remains with me just a couple of feet away from my desk. The musical scores are ready to reveal his world to me over and over, and over again.

I no longer live on Granger Street.

In memory of Lukas Foss

The Not So Short Walk

Linda Orrell-Fair

Many years ago, when our children were young, my sister and I spent wonderful times at our cottage on Keuka Lake. Our mother and aunt were also there. We spent enjoyable family time all summer long.

Since the children were old enough to be semi-independent, and there were other adults around, my sister and I would take a walk after dinner. One evening we started out, but did not take the usual route. That's when things got interesting!

We headed up the hill from the main road. Less than an eighth of a mile up the road there was a bridge with a creek running under it. The creek obviously ran downhill and into the lake. So we said to each other why not walk down the creek bed, and head home that way? It would be more interesting than on a flat road. Her old dog was also with us. There was not much water, and we had walked many creeks so there should have been no problem. As we hiked along, we realized that an eighth of a mile up doesn't necessarily mean an eighth of a mile down. This creek turned to the left, then went way back to the right, then left again, and right again. It not only meandered all over the hillside but was very steep in some places. This was not a flat creek bed like we expected it to be. There were many cliffs that were difficult to maneuver so we could get down. Not only for us but also her dog. Many times, we had to lift the dog off a rock ledge. She was not a small dog! This walk took much longer than we expected and we were concerned Mom would be worried. It was almost dark when we reached the main road. The shocking thing was when we walked into the cottage no one had missed us!

[I worked for Wayne Finger Lakes BOCES as a Special Education teacher. Now that I am retired, I enjoy relaxing at my home on Keuka Lake and spending time with my sister and with my grandchildren,]

An Uninvited Guest

Jean Trost

The six of us were gathered around the grill in the back yard, talking and watching the whitefish and salmon be transformed into our dinner. We were still in bathing suits, drying out. We had spent the entire day in and near the lake, on the wooden deck by the water.

We noticed an uninvited guest arriving from the lakeside. He was walking (waddling?) along the Lilac bushes that lined the side of the yard. He passed by the cottage and came nearer.

What was a seagull doing so close to us? He probably wanted some of that fish he smelled. He seemed unafraid yet desperate.

Then we noticed that something was wrong with him. As he came closer, we saw that he was all tangled up with a fisherman's line around his beak and back. He couldn't eat – and hadn't for how long? Obviously, he couldn't fly either. It was like he was coming to us for help.

A plan was quickly developed. Jenny got a towel and sharp scissors. Rubber gloves would have been nice in case of biting, but we couldn't find them. From behind him, she wrapped the towel around him as he tried to flap his wings.

Linda grabbed his beak and courageously held it while Sue cut the lines that bound it closed. Then she moved on to the ones around his neck and back. We worried that there might be a hook imbedded in his throat, but couldn't tell.

Next, the rest of us threw bits of fish toward him. (We now called him Henry.) We got him a glass of water. He couldn't get any, so a deeper glass was secured. This, he was able to manage better.

By this time, our dinner was ready. We left him to eat and drink in peace and went inside. Later, we saw him walking toward the lake and then across a neighbor's lawn to the beach.

We promised ourselves we'd call the Fish and Game Service in the morning if he was still around. We didn't find him again. Perhaps we should have called them right away, but we acted instinctively out of pity.

We wonder if he's alive or dead, rejoined with his buddies or all alone.

Oh, Henry!

Jean Trost has written stories for tutors to use through Writers for Literacy and is active in Canandaigua's Wood Library and her church.

Angel Unaware

By Mike Wischnowski

"Do not neglect to show hospitality to strangers, for thereby some have entertained angels unawares."

—*Hebrews 13:2*

On my morning walk, I found a wallet. It was toward the end of the walk, tramping downhill on the country road near our complex. Gravity-assisted, the descent was easier than the earlier tread up the hill, my breathing steadier, but the strain in my knees increased as my stride lengthened and quickened as the momentum pulled me toward the bottom. I had dressed too warmly in a sweat suit and jacket for this early summer day and neglected to grab my hat and sunglasses. The sun had come out with increased intensity, evaporating last night's rain, its rays penetrating, bearing down on what might become a headache.

And there it was. In a few more paces, I would have been off the road and onto our more suburban street unencumbered, but in a split second my eye detected the incongruity of the black lump lying in the rain-flattened weeds on the side of the road, something obviously different from the rocks or occasional litter one would expect and pass by. I stopped to make sure I was seeing what I was seeing and already knowing, hesitated to pick it up, sensing trouble, more responsibility inside of it.

But, how can you not pick up a wallet?

The instant detection of money always surprises me, the quickness with which the brain absorbs the possibility of unearned gain, the reflexive adherence to the childish law of finders-keepers, the providence of it, these thoughts all wrapped up in milliseconds.

I remembered stopping at an intersection years ago as a much younger man, suddenly seeing multiple, green papers scudding in the wind like dried-up leaves, parade-like, in front of me, the street oddly empty, and I knew immediately, unmistakably, those were dollars. I shifted the car in park with a jerk, and chased down nearly a hundred bucks in multiple denominations, not believing my good fortune. I was out of and back in the car in less than two minutes and made my getaway. Breathing heavily, wracked with adrenalin, my teeth clenched in good fortune, I didn't even look in the direction of where the money may have come from. I avoided the rear-view mirror, glancing regularly, proudly at the pile of balled-up loot in the passenger's seat.

It's mine, I thought. All mine.

As my breathing became more regular and I met the speed limit again, I returned to the scene in my mind. There had been a tavern, a dive, on one of the corners and I imagined a drunk walking toward its entrance, a freshly cashed check blowing out of his pockets. A tinge of remorse, a Christian road not taken, seeped into my exhilaration: a glimpse of the drunk's family doing without a week's worth of groceries. I made mental justifications. He would probably have drunk it away anyway.

Considering now this wallet on the side of the road, I told myself that I was an older, richer, less greedy man now, more attune to the karma, the trickle effect, of lost, found, unreturned things. I stepped off the road and into the wet weeds. The sole of my sneaker lost traction and I almost fell. Catching my balance, I took a look around to see if anyone was watching me. I picked up the wallet delicately, as if it could be contaminated. I recalled my parents cautioning me as a child: "Never pick up anything off the street. You never know where it's been!"

The wallet was made of worn, brown leather, browner, almost black from the rain. A moist, skin-like covering tightening around something more solid inside, it was about the size of a human heart. I unfolded it and was confronted with the driver's license of its owner, his face incarcerated behind a plastic, mesh screen, a middle-aged man, long hair in an outdated, 1970's style, but needing a cut, bangs coming too far over the lenses of his aviator glasses and the hair on the sides mid-ear-length. A bit of glare on the glasses, the face was slightly perturbed, maybe from having been in a line too long at the DMV. A working man's face, I thought, a little defeated-looking.

On the opposite side, squeezed into their slots, were a Visa card, a debit card from a local bank, and a big box membership card. Holding my breath, I opened the sleeve where cash would have been, its lining frayed, the space incriminatingly empty.

If there was cash in it, in that moment, would I have taken it? Completed the crime? Thrown the wallet back into the weeds?

There was another slot behind the credit card pockets and I found a mashed stack of five or so wet business cards there. The man's name was Dan Josefsen, Kitchen and Bathroom Remodeling. There was a picture of a spic-and-span kitchen with a sparkle like a star coming off one of the cabinets, a P.O. Box, the name of the town we both lived in, a phone number. Standing up from my crouch, sweating under the new day sun, I looked again to see if anyone was watching me. Insanely, I worried about how I would fit this into my schedule. I was tempted to leave well enough alone; however, I knew what was expected of me, walked home with the wallet, still holding it delicately, and got ready for work.

⌇

I waited until I was settled in my office, knocked off some leftover concerns from the day before, and called Mr. Josefsen at a reasonable, mid-morning hour. After a few rings, he answered, his hello sounding a little groggy, some twangy music in the background that took a bit to turn down. He sounded older than his DMV picture and became more alert if not a little sheepish once he knew the reason for my call. I heard my own voice become very business-like, like one you hear on the radio, a cadence that needs to make a good first impression. Trustworthy, I hoped.

"Oh my God...," he started. "Well, thank you, sir, for picking it up and calling me." He spoke to a woman in the background, the rush of water running in a bucket in a sink. "Someone found my wallet." "Oh!" I heard her shout with surprise and relief, as if a prayer were suddenly answered. I told him where I found it, that his license, the credit and debit card were still in it, but there was no cash.

A pause.

"Well," he said. "I was in a work accident about six months ago. Fell off a goddam ladder. Busted up one arm real bad. Broke a few ribs. Still recovering. Go to PT almost every day still." A puff from a cigarette. "I wear these darn sweat pants when I go there. It's easier to do the rehab in them, but they have the shallowest of pockets. I think the wallet must have fallen out in the hospital parking lot."

He paused again, took a slurp of coffee. I think he was waiting for me to say something.

"Oh," I said. "That sounds rough. Sorry that's happened to you." After that sounding like not quite genuine, I added: "I hope the rehab's working."

"Oh, man," a puckering sound around a cigarette, "I been off work all of this time driving this woman crazy. I think somebody picked it up, saw there was little or no cash in it, I can't remember exactly. Figured credit and debit cards weren't worth it, and just threw it out the window on their way home. Being the Good Samaritan like you was apparently out of the question once they had already considered the alternative."

My assistant appeared behind the window in my office door and pointed to her watch. I recovered my radio voice to keep the conversation transactional. "Can you drive? Do you want to meet somewhere this evening?" Still, that irritation, wanting out of this... "I'm up in the city and won't be able to get back to town until about eight-thirty tonight. Do you want to meet in the McDonald's parking lot, near the lake?"

"Um, ok, um," slowly to his wife: "Hon, can I have the car to go pick up the wallet at McDonald's tonight?" I hear a woman's mumble and assent, and a warning to be careful. Back to me: "Yeah, that will be ok." He sounded more guarded, as if I was putting them out some, like I should meet at a more convenient time and place for them or maybe it was just a sense of stranger-danger coming out.

"We'll work it out."

"Ok, then," I said. "I have a silver-colored Audi." And for some God-forsaken reason had to add: "I'll be wearing a suit."

"Huh," he said, considering this. "Ok, then. See you at the McDonald's. Thank you again for your good-heartedness."

"No problem," I lied. "See you at McDonald's at 8:30." He said,

"Goodbye" and not thinking I said "Bye-bye" in the way I always end calls from family or friends, compensating.

※

I am at the age where I theoretically could retire, but the actual number doesn't quite conform to the government-sanctioned milestones of Medicare or Social Security, and I am nothing if not a conformist. I am a Vice-President for Finance at a private Christian college. A little unorthodox, I started at the college as a Finance professor first, played the academic game, and achieved tenure in six years. My dissertation and later research studied the effects on lenders of unpaid Federal student loans offered to undergraduates in the 1970's. I predicted the unintended consequences of stricter policy measures and the debt crisis we see on today's students and families. I was one of those 1970's college students who received a full-tuition state scholarship and one of those generous Federal loans back then, qualifying as an oldest child of a single mother raising six kids alone and a deadbeat dad.

With a vengeance, I paid my loan back in full, on time.

For some ungodly reason, I left my tenured position to become the VP, a position in which I learned to be proficient and secured for myself and my family an upper-middle-class existence. But, as I've gotten older, I have to admit, it's felt in many ways like a serious life misstep, going from almost daily affirmation in the classroom with my mostly adoring students to a zero-based-budget imposer on my colleagues, doling out myself or managing departments that regularly dole out belt-tightening news to the Deans and Directors, my overworked staff often functioning as collection agencies for hapless students and families. I keep the construction of donor-named dormitories and academic buildings, of which there has been considerable in my time here, as the President says, "on time and on budget." I have a critical role in the operation that has become increasingly powerful, but also extremely isolating. There's been a lot of turnover in my division. Yet, my job is secure. The College is solvent, has good credit, carries a reasonable amount of debt, enjoys a growing endowment, and we've invested enough in the place, in our "brand", to stay ahead of demographic, political, and social headwinds that have found and devastated other Christian institutions of our kind.

More and more, I can't help thinking each day that my work is done here.

On the home front, with our children raised and married and out of town, my wife and I both work ridiculous hours and largely stay out of each other's way. The empty nest is usually empty, except for some late meals and sleeping. We are both gaining weight, computer-bound in both of our jobs, no time for exercise, neither of us happy with the way our clothes fit us now. We recognize and assure ourselves that we are both in a holding pattern until retirement comes. We will take better care of ourselves when we get there, we think, when there will be more time.

After calling Mr. Josefsen, I had a budget meeting with one of the Deans, someone who started here about the same time as I did, who like me was once a popular professor who climbed one more wrung of the ladder, "went to the dark side" of administration as the faculty say, and likewise made himself considerably more financially comfortable and psychologically more miserable. A face with a smile once full of hope and encouragement for striving young people, his brow is now furrowed, his shoulders stooped, his mouth closed tight like one cornered and not knowing what to do. Unlike in most other parts of the college, enrollment has fallen steadily in his School and each year has brought at least one layoff of non-tenured faculty or staff positions, people who actually did their work in many cases, and a decreased operational budget. I feel for him, brighten up with him when he musters up his old happy-go-lucky self, but finally stare at him with the dead-eyed face of a mob boss when the data speaks for itself. He leaves, trying hard not to reveal how shook he is, making him look all the more shook.

These meetings take their toll on both of us. We were both something else once, maybe better versions of ourselves, breathing better air, even teaching outside sometimes on the better spring and autumn days, and now here we are in my dim, musty Old Main office, phony golf paraphernalia on the walls from various tournament fundraisers, a couple of trophies (my team was better than I was, but I display them anyway) on a file cabinet, the two of us, torturer and tortured, in the budget dance.

It makes me question my entire education.

After he left, I climbed the steep stairway (it seems steeper every day) to the fourth floor where the men's lavatory is and some of the smaller, forgotten departments (philosophy; religious studies; economics) with doddering professors in cramped, worn-carpeted, musty-book-lined offices once seminary bedrooms, some with old, wooden crucifixes still affixed to the walls. I go into the stall, even though I only have to pee, and I relieve myself, crouched, catching my breath.

My evening dinner is in one of the oldest country clubs in the city, its charms including an old indoor pool that some old-timers still use and which gives the whole place an underlying scent of chlorine and mildew. The club, now sprawling due to decade-after-decade additions paid for with increasingly expensive membership dues, ones that have excluded generations of questionable riff-raff (like myself not that long ago), can't shake, actually basks, in its own historical fustiness . The newest addition, built last year, is an expansive dining room attached to a modernized kitchen complete with a gourmet chef recently relocated from Las Vegas. It still feels like an appendage, like it doesn't belong here.

Once you exit from the new dining room you can feel the decades go by in each receding section—a spa with five massage rooms and large salt water hot tub and sauna; a business center with a computer lab and rarely used printers; a bar with a disco ball over its square of polished dance floor; another dining room that looks out over and intimidates many golfers on Hole #9; another bar with bar food and a TV patrons can look up to as if baseball and boxing still mattered; a workout room that leads to a newer outdoor pool; and then a wheelchair ramp next to stairs that brings one into the old mansion starting with a 1920's ballroom to the right with art deco stylings still useful for larger functions

The side entrance to the house here still has an overhang, a canopy that always gives me the sense that the place was once a funeral parlor, horse-drawn hearses seeking shelter underneath it to bring caskets in from the rain. Stairs lead you to a hall with an umbrella stand I always notice and wonder the last time I used an umbrella. There is an untouched windowless, billiard room, the tables morgue-like, covered in faded green sheaths, dust in the light of the overhanging lamps meandering like ghosts, mocking the once smoke-fueled air of men only. Across the hall to the left is a library with books only for show now, maybe always just for show. There is a music room with a piano in it, also covered, and a little stage; there is a kitchen and old dining room now partitioned off into staff offices. The walls in this area are decorated with the photos of dead robber barons, I presume, supposedly former pillars of the community going back more than a century, whose first names I imagine to be Abner or Phineas.

You could murder Professor Plum with a candlestick in the fucking conservatory here.

Climbing upstairs by way of a curved, carpeted, but groaning staircase (there is no elevator here, the place stubbornly inaccessible), the College's Senior Staff meet for retreat-like, special meetings, always in the same room, some dead titan's bedroom once, I imagine. They've kept up the Gilded Age by way of Jazz Age décor in here—furniture with animal-clawed legs, lamps with tassels on their shades, wallpaper with enormous flowers in bloom, a deer head, shot long ago, looking innocent and dead-eyed over all the proceedings. My yearly budget "retreat" is held in this room. We ruin the whole effect with our laptops and the projector (which never seems to focus on my Excel sheets right) and a screen we supply ourselves for our Power Points of data. We are like visitors from the future, from the end of time.

Tonight is a retirement dinner, held in the ballroom, for one of the College's Board of Trustee members. One of the parts of my job that I have never quite mastered is the glad-handing. I get by. The Board and the President depend on me to be the wizard with the figures; if I have a sparkling personality beyond that, I think it almost makes me suspect, so I tuck away part of the spirit I know I once had and stay interpersonally within the margins, mostly speak when spoken to, seek out the others who share my upper-mid-level standing, mostly the other VPs and some of the bankers and public officials I work regularly with from the Board. I'm enough of a working-class kid to still be intimidated in a country club, my not belonging transparent I suspect, here only because of my indirect association with a member who can afford it. God bless the child indeed.

If I drink too much at these things, my wife has told me that I step out a little too recklessly and I'm likely to say something I will regret later, so I've learned to order a tonic water or club soda. It looks like I'm drinking what the others are, but I'm not.

Flying solo (Angie at her own function somewhere), I am assigned a seat between two wives of two Trustees at a circular table for eight, Angie's table setting removed. I often do better with the women than the men at these things, but that is not the case tonight. The women want to talk with each other and I am in the way. I carefully eat my salad from a few inches too far from the table so the women can converse, bowing into the salad occasionally like a supplicant, getting a bite in when they pause in their conversation, trying not to get dressing on myself. I comment when it would be impossible not to, but I am mostly not here.

The dinner food is rich and delicious (a filet mignon, mashed potatoes, and asparagus... Not sure if this one thing is a garnish or if I should eat it. I decide to leave it alone.) The wife to my right orders a vegan plate and the rest of the table surmises it rather curiously and weighs its significance to their own. I eat everything on my plate, eat dessert while the retiree is being touted and mildly roasted (the audience's "ha,ha,ha" coming from not quite deep enough in the throat, not anywhere near the heart), and time my fast track to the exit.

Once outside, the humid summer air relaxes and soothes my body's tenseness from the chilly, recirculated air-conditioning inside. (Both wives said they wished they'd brought a sweater, but a sweater would have ruined their bare-armed, short-skirted outfits. I didn't believe them for a minute.)

I give the nervous, acned valet my ticket, probably some club member's son, and close my eyes, waiting anxiously for my car. When it comes, I shake hands with and over-tip the valet, my brother in social anxiety, and am grateful to get back in my Audi, put on my classic rock and shades, and head for McDonalds.

"Thanks, sir," the valet said. "Nice ride."

I arrive in the McDonalds parking lot, with ten minutes to spare before my meeting time with Dan. The over-extended sun is out, but beginning its decline, a church steeple in silhouette reaching up above the city, a few clouds, a few black birds, the sky still blue, the houses below it already dark. Late for the sky. Little by little, the McDonalds' light will become dominant out here. In the humid evening air, the smell of French Fries mixed with some of the garbage out back permeates. Some June bugs are out, occasionally lighting on my windshield, bouncing around with some moths near the electric sign.

Not knowing quite what to do while waiting, I get out of the car and walk into the restaurant, on the chance that Josefsen is waiting in there. I don't see anyone quite matching his DMV photo, but am surprised at how busy the place is; a lot of people still getting supper or nursing the latest ice cream concoctions. I've already eaten too much tonight, almost order a sundae, but think better of it. A couple of plastic-boothed patrons notice me. I draw suspicion.

I return to the car and wait, electronically I bring the front windows down, get a cross-breeze. A gaggle of high school kids, maybe ten of them, their cars and trucks lined up at a distance from me in the lot, talk and laugh loudly, boys and girls together. The scene reminds me of my high school days and I am frankly surprised to see young people forming community around their chariots like this, like we used to. I thought the phones and video games had taken over, this generation sensually blocked from each other by the social media. In the 70's, a car's eight-track player would have been blaring. There is music here tonight, too, classic rock (How about that?) coming from a truck's radio. Bad Company. The scene, the music, the summer night with plenty more ahead of them: I wonder if retirement will be anything like high school.

Gulls from the lake investigate the lot's scrap possibilities, teenagers they surmise an easy mark. Without fear, they inspect the lot near the kids with comic military bearing, and squawk and shriek their orders. A pretty girl throws a French fry at one of the noisier ones and it gobbles the fry as fast as it can, other birds flying in fast to steal it or reap from the next tossing. This is hilarious to the girl, pretty in her long black hair parted down the middle, smock-y top, skinny jeans, and sandals. Everything old is new again. She gets her peer group to focus on the scavengers while she tosses more fries.

One boy says: "I'll take those if you don't want them. I haven't had dinner." The girl tosses a French fry his way and he catches it in his mouth like one of the more agile birds. They all applaud and say hooray, give the kid a fake, affectionate, hard time.

I pick up an occasional curse word from one of the boys said with emphasis. It is free sounding, coming out unusual in the teen's mouth, he finally owning it, it seems, a declaration of independence. One of the girls screams in absolute horror or ecstasy or both, but then chases it with an exaggerated laugh, actually enjoying the grab-ass or whatever illicit touch elicited this equal declaration. I find myself smiling, enjoying the bits of adolescent chatter among the power chords, the fresh bonding with its own exciting soundtrack that was so intoxicating back then. For a moment, I thought of my friends, my girlfriends, our old cars and trucks, our secret crushes on each other, my popular status in the group. I let myself feel it. Nostalgia, neuralgia... I put my head on the steering wheel and closed my eyes. I'm really tired, I thought.

Still waiting to return the wallet... I decide to take my post outside the car, standing next on the driver's side in my summer suit, now rumpled and ill-fitting, not bothering to button the jacket that hides my own spare tire. Forthrightly holding the wallet I think will make me instantly recognizable to Josefsen and would appear to have the desired effect of communicating the efficiency I want with this transaction. It also strikes me that this could look like a drug deal or some sort of weird pick-up.

No. I'm just standing up, I tell myself. Upstanding. Ha! Trying to do the right thing. Hurry up!

I concentrate on the kids and gulls, a nature documentary with a satisfyingly, almost prurient close angle. I seem invisible to them. I deeply want to join them.

I look up, beyond the plastic golden light of the sign, up into the natural light of the stars twinkling like cow eyes in a night field. I stretch, make a Y with my body, sneak in another prayer, holding the wallet as an offering.

⎯⎯

"TO BE A ROCK AND NOT TO ROOOHHLLLLLLLlllllll...," soulfully mourns Robert Plant, and "Stairway to Heaven" for maybe the thousandth time in my life (still don't know what it all means) makes its way to its denouement, the sonic wall of guitars and drums and bass finally exhausted after their transcendent crescendo, letting it all peter out, leaving Plant, last man standing, barely eking out the final tragic phrase (Why was this song so tragic?), a slowly gasping, mysterious 'Rosebud':

"And she's buy-uy-ing the stair-er-way... to hea-vonnnn..."

My head is down; I'm almost sleeping on my feet. I am looking at Dan's wallet, how the impression of the credit card is visible in its shrunken skin and feeling its heart-like weight again in my hand. I take out my own wallet, split it open and choose the hundred-dollar bill I'd been carrying around for a while, waiting for the right opportunity to spend it. I fold and shove the bill into the slot where the mashed, sopping business cards had been.

When I look up, the pretty girl who fed the birds was running toward me. "Mister," she shouts to me as if she knew me, a serious look on her face, her youth and beauty jarring, seeming almost impossible. "Do you have any jumper cables? One of us needs a start."

"All of those cars and trucks, and no one has cables?" Grouchy. What is my problem?

"No," she says assuredly, and then smiles, figuring there had to be a helpful person in me somewhere. Where do these kids get their confidence these days?

"Just a minute." I throw Dan's wallet in the front seat and open my trunk with the fob. The snake-like red and black cables with the small copper teeth usually in with the spare was missing. Now where did that go? "I'm sorry," I say. "I spoke too soon. Someone must have taken them." Angie? I put my hands in the trunk and pretend to rummage the nothingness to better prove my point. "I can't give you a boost." A terrible sadness comes over me like failure, a missed opportunity.

"That's ok," she says, seeing my sadness. "We'll find someone."

She smiles again and dashes off, stops herself and shouts, "Thanks for looking."

Just then, an old Dodge (A Duster?) pulls into the lot and in the driver's seat is Dan Josefsen, looking just like his picture, only older, grayer, unshaven, the same glasses, maybe a stronger prescription. He moseys out of his car in obvious pain, rocking back and forth for the final thrust up, and stands up to about my height, and asks my name. He is wearing a faded "Life is Good" tee-shirt with a campfire on it and a pair of black sweat pants, maybe the ones the wallet slipped out of in the first place.

"That's me," I say, back to my business-like efficiency and step forward to shake his offered left hand with my right, his casted right hand held back so I wouldn't be tempted, his left forearm branded with a tattoo of a heart with a knife through it.

I hand over the wallet. He says sort of sheepish, "Thank you. You've saved me a lot of trouble with those credit cards." He instinctively looks in the sleeve, saw that the cash that was never there was still missing, and makes sure that the cards were in place and (I hold my breath) doesn't fish any further. He shoves the wallet into his left sweat pants pocket which seems to have a hard time bearing the wallet's weight. Someone else is going to need to find that wallet for him again, I bet.

"I would give you something for your trouble," starts Dan sympathetically.

I make a hand motion, the universal sign for "Don't worry about it." "You made my day, Dan," I say. I notice when I say that to people they usually like the sound of it.

Dan considers the remark and chuckles. "OK then," he says. "Thanks again." We both look away as if the moment calls for something more from us, but we can't think of what it is. I shake his left hand again and walk toward my driver's side door and do think of something.

"Hey, Dan, do you have any jumper cables?"

He has his first foot onto the floor of the driver's side of the Duster, starting the arduous way back into the driver's seat.

"Sure," he says. "Need a boost?"

I explain the situation and he opens his trunk with a key. The space is surprisingly neat and practical—a first-aid kit, a toolbox, blankets, a cooler, and jumper cables—and we walk over to the pretty girl who points out which car needs a boost. The long-haired boy, who I gather is her boyfriend, embarrassed to be needy, opens the hood and smelling the engine's oily aroma I do what Dan would have done with his cables, connect to another car whose battery is not dead, and the dead car comes back to life. "Give it some gas," Dan shouts. He seems to enjoy the instructional part of this.

Led by the pretty girl, the kids clap and say hooray, and thank us, the long-haired boy behind the wheel, getting out of the car, comes right up to the pretty girl and gives her a tender kiss of gratitude, for bringing helpers to the scene and maybe something more. I am oddly proud of myself, making a Rube Goldberg contraption in my head that started with a wallet on the side of the road and now ending with an expression of love. It started even before that.

Happy to be an admired part of this group if just for a few minutes, I bask under the light, but remember not to linger and free the cables from the battery, a little spark jumping off the battery and burning a small spot on my suit coat. "So long. You're welcome. Get some cables."

Walking back, I slow down my gait so Dan can keep up. I notice some grease and grime from the car on my white shirt and suit jacket and pants. I finally take the jacket off and throw it into my back seat. Why was I wearing it all this time?

"You sure made my day, Mister," Dan says, stealing my line and showing me the wallet, and we both chuckle. Even Steven, I think.

"OH...MY...GOD," shrieks one of the high school girls. Other girls chime in with their own feigned outrage and it all spilled over into pure adolescent hilarity and joy. Dan and I turn briefly to see what the matter is and realize nothing is the matter. One boy laughs hard and turns around in circles he is so overcome.

Dan struggles back into his car and I wait until he is settled. We drive slowly out of the parking lot, me following Dan, leaving the teenagers, bathed in the golden light, in our rearview mirrors.

And as we wind on down the road, I think, not tragically, "It's time for me to retire."

No Ordinary First Lady

Jewel Wink

History came alive on a recent trip while visiting the presidential library and homestead of Franklin Roosevelt in Hyde Park. It was striking to see the similarity of turbulent issues faced by FDR and to compare them to the critical challenges we face today.

But in reflection, Val Kill, Eleanor Roosevelt's nearby cottage home in Hyde Park held the greatest fascination as she has long been my heroine. This first lady combined modesty, compassion, intelligence, wit and a fervent commitment to the greater good. With FDR's infirmities, she became his legs —visiting coal mines, tasting the soup in the soup kitchens, eating with soldiers at the mess hall and traveling the world as an ambassador. She saw firsthand the needy and oppressed which she reported back to her husband.

Her impressions and assessments became the foundations of critical changes and innovative policies. She instigated a national consciousness as she exposed incidents of racism on a moral and legal basis.

"We can treat others with respect due to all human beings and we will receive respect in return, regardless of race, color or creed." E. Roosevelt

We can only imagine her reaction to our President Elect.

Throughout her public life the press ridiculed her for her appearance and social activism. Yet she sought to improve at every turn even to the smallest detail of taking voice lessons to smooth her delivery.

"...words can be the cruelest of weapons." E. Roosevelt

A gracious hostess, her home at Val Kill reflects the First Lady's penchant for comfort and simplicity. Chairs of every size, shape and softness centered around the fireplace in the small living room to accommodate the preferences of her many guests. She used everyday china and plain glassware to create a warm atmosphere. The press had a heyday when they learned she had served the King and Queen of England hot dogs picnic style.

At a modest table in the corner of the living room, she had tea with an eager Senator John F. Kennedy seeking and receiving her endorsement for his candidacy for president. His Catholicism was perceived as a stumbling block for his presidency —fodder for the politicos of the time. Mrs. Roosevelt was appalled by these attacks.

Along with family photos, pictures displayed her proudest moments such as when the United Nations Universal Declaration of Human Rights was drafted as a result of her leadership as Chairman of the UN Commission on Human Rights. She has been named the Woman of the Century in a survey by the Woman's National Hall of Fame.

> *"We must regain a vision of ourselves as leaders of the world. We must join in an effort to use all knowledge for the good of all human beings. When we do that, we shall have nothing to fear."* E. Roosevelt

I picked up a book in the gift shop entitled MY DAY, which included Mrs. Roosevelt's newspaper columns from 1935-1962. Her perceptions gave the public a day to day window into the happenings of the White House and further to the spirit of the First Lady: Astounding accomplishments held by a woman with a strange voice, frumpy appearance and sensible shoes.

Eleanor and FDR gave *hope* to a downtrodden America. Perhaps we can rekindle the lesson from history that *substance* matters.

The "Y"

Jenny Mahoney

It was one of those perfect days in Paradise. The tide was out and there wasn't a cloud in the sky as the sun rose over the Mokulua Islands painting the pure white sands in various hues of gold and pink. Lori Franklin and Julie Ward rose early on Saturday morning, hoping to beat any of the neighbors who might also be walking the beach in search of glass balls. These blown glass balls, which originated as floats on the nets of Japanese fishermen, were highly sought after by beach lovers of all ages. They'd travelled for years over thousands of miles and came in many shapes, sizes and colors. Some were encrusted with shells or coral and some were even filled with water. The water apparently seeped in from tiny cracks when the ball was forced down into the ocean by some mysterious force of nature. It's amazing that any of them survived the trip. But survive they did – by the hundreds! Lori had found two so far, but her mother and younger sister (who were much more committed to early rising) had found about 20 over the past two years.

Lori usually slept in until at least 7:00 a.m., but today was special.

Her best friend, Julie, had joined her on the bus home from school Friday afternoon and was spending the weekend, as she did most weekends. They had hatched the plan yesterday afternoon as they floated on the water in the huge airplane inner tube Lori's father had obtained from Hickam Air Base near Pearl Harbor. This was their routine. Every Friday after the two got home from school, they would head to the beach with the inner tube and spend about two hours swimming, sunning and singing at the top of their lungs as they floated in the calm waters off Lanikai Beach. It was the 13th of December 1963 and time was running out for them to get their Christmas shopping done. As it happened, Lori's mother and a neighborhood friend were going into Honolulu the next day for their bi-weekly art class at the YWCA. The girls figured they could catch a ride into the city and spend a couple of hours shopping downtown before meeting up with Lori's mother at the end of her class. The class was held from 9:00 a.m. to 12:00 noon and Mrs. Franklin planned to leave promptly at 8:15 a.m.

After walking the length of the beach and back with no luck on the ball hunting, the girls arrived home and quickly dressed for the day. By 7:30 a.m. they were sitting at the kitchen counter enjoying a light breakfast of fresh papaya and lemon. By 8:00 a.m. they had finished eating, brushed their teeth and were ready to go. Lori had a special request. "Mom, I know there will only be four of us in the car, but can we sit in the rumble seat?" Normally, Lori's mother preferred her children to sit in the middle seat of the 1960 Ford Fairlane station wagon which she felt offered more protection in the event of an accident. Her mother frowned briefly, but then relented when she saw the hopeful look on the girls' faces.

The girls climbed into the rumble seat and Mrs. Franklin closed the back door. They both loved riding in the back. It gave them an interesting backward perspective of the scenery as it unfolded, but more importantly, it provided better privacy for their highly secretive girl talk. They had known each other for almost ten years, having met as first graders. Now sophomores in high school they were still very best friends and, as usual, had plenty to talk about.

By 8:20 they had picked up their fourth passenger and were heading toward the Pali Highway. As their car made its way up the valley towards the twin tunnels which would take them through the Koolau Range into Honolulu, the panoramic view of the town of Kailua and the windward side of Oahu slowly spread out below them. They could see the twin Mokulua islands which sat a mile offshore of the very beach they were walking along that morning. The beach itself was a bright white strip which stood out against the turquoise blue/green of the bay. Scanning to the left was the U.S. Marine base at Kaneohe which occupied a narrow isthmus between the town of Kailua and the jutting Ulupau head. As their car rose higher, more of the windward side of Oahu came into view. Far to the left they could make out Chinaman's Hat – the small island that looked exactly like its namesake and marked the gateway to the North Shore and big surf country. To their right, the forefront was dominated by Mount

Before I Forget

Olomana, the large three peaked hill that was popular with hikers. Directly below them, the town of Kailua with its few tall buildings seemed to fade into the surrounding lush greenery of local banana and papaya farms. At the very foot of the Koolau Range sat the Pali Golf Course - its fairways, putting greens and sand traps enhancing the intriguing tapestry of the countryside. In their peripheral vision, the girls were aware of the imposing Koolau Mountain Range looming above and then enveloping them. This bright green range was particularly striking today as the knife sharp ridges and peaks stood out so sharply against the cloudless blue sky. Lori never tired of these mountains – especially up close to them as she was now. She imagined some giant in eons past picking up a huge lump of clay and molding the mountain range by raking his fingers down the sides of the mound of clay and gouging out the succession of spiny ridges that marched in a towering line down the center of the island.

"Tunnel 1 – hold your breath" Julie called out breaking into Lori's reverie. They both held their breath as they entered the first tunnel. They emerged about ten seconds later and quickly sucked in their breath again as they entered the longer second tunnel. This was a bit more of a challenge – they would have to hold their breath for almost half a minute to make it through the second tunnel. "Did you make a wish?" asked Lori as they exited the second tunnel. "Not worth it", said Julie. "It's not even a challenge. The Wilson Tunnel is much tougher. You have to hold your breath for almost a minute!"

They had exited the two tunnels into the verdant Nuuanu Valley.

The girls admired the lush foliage and many waterfalls as the gentler grade of the highway on the leeward side of the mountain range slowly lowered them to the valley floor and the outskirts of the city of Honolulu. They soon passed the Board of Water Supply which was naturally dressed for the holiday season with its beautiful hedge of red Poinsettia's ablaze along the front of the building.

The sight of the festive Christmas flowers prompted the girls to start singing Mele Kalimaka (Hawaii's Christmas song), which was followed by a number of other Christmas carols they had been practicing for the upcoming Kailua High School Christmas concerts. Both Lori and Julie had successfully auditioned for the Kailua High Select Chorus, which meant that their choral robes were adorned with white bands around the sleeves and they were placed in the front row of the choir whenever they performed a concert. Kailua High's famous Madrigal singers were selected from this group and they often accompanied the Madrigals to performances throughout the island. They were both looking forward to getting out of class next Wednesday to travel to the North Shore for a concert at Kahuku High School.

Lori still couldn't believe she had made it into the Select Chorus. For years she had tried out for various choral groups and was always rejected. In 6th grade, she was actually the **only** student in her class that was not selected for the Christmas Chorus. The difference at Kailua High was that the school was blessed with a truly outstanding choral director. Mr. Hotoke could teach anyone how to sing and was very committed to his students. He often invited students to stay after class for private coaching lesson. Lori had taken advantage of this offer a number of times. She soon learned that she was a natural Alto and that her problem in the past was that she was trying to sing the Soprano part in an Alto voice. Julie, on the other hand, had a beautiful Soprano voice and together they harmonized their way through the first three songs of the upcoming Christmas program.

They were about to start on the "Hallelujah Chorus" when Mrs. Franklin called out, "We're coming to the corner of Fort Street and Beretania – I'll pull over so you can get out here". "Do you know how to get to the YWCA?" she asked as the car pulled to a stop. "Oh sure" said Lori. "I know the building; we pass it every time we come into Honolulu". "OK" continued her mother. "Be sure to meet us there no later than noon. The class is held on the third floor; just come straight up on the elevator. You can't miss the classroom."

The girls got out of the car and headed down Fort Street, Honolulu's downtown shopping district. There were three major department stores – Liberty House, Kress and Woolworths – but they were more interested in checking out the several small retail shops which carried unique gifts from Hawaii and around the world including Japan and the Philippines. Julie was nuts about anything Japanese and Lori leaned towards some of the local Hawaiian handicrafts. They walked the length of Fort Street, popping into several shops and making quite a dent in their respective Christmas lists. Julie found a lovely Japanese figurine for her mother, while Lori chose a Kukui Nut necklace for hers. They both struggled with gifts for their fathers, but found several items for their sisters. For her youngest sister, Lori bought a couple of boxes of Tomoe Ame candy at the cracked seed store. A favorite with the locals, this sweet gummy candy from Japan was wrapped in edible rice paper – you literally popped the whole thing in your mouth and the wrapper would melt away as the sweet taste of the candy oozed into your mouth. Before leaving the store, she decided to pick up an extra box for herself and both girls were unable to resist the selection of cracked seed and See Mui. These dried fruit snacks were brought over to Hawaii in the 1800's by Chinese field laborers. There were many varieties, but most of them were made from dried plums and all of them were salty enough to make your mouth pucker. Lori's favorite was the Li Hing Mui, which had just the right combination of saltiness and sweetness. Julie preferred the cracked seed, which was wetter and sweeter but the inner stone was indeed cracked and the little bits and pieces were a nuisance when they got stuck in your teeth.

Their shopping done for the day, the girls walked back up Fort Street and turned onto Beretania. The "Y" was about two blocks down, an imposing five story Spanish style building with a circular driveway and lovely manicured grounds. They walked up the front steps and took the elevator to the third floor. As they stepped off the elevator they were surprised to see a layout that looked more like a hotel than a classroom setting. There was a walkway all around the inside perimeter of the building and you could look down from the half wall of the walkway and see the lobby below. On the outside of the walkway there were a series of doors which obviously led to individual rooms much too small to house an art class. Across the open space they could see men's underwear hanging out to dry on the half wall of the walkway on the other side of the building.

"This doesn't look right", said Lori. Maybe we should ask those guys over there." She pointed out two young men who were standing outside one of the doorways about half way up their wing of the walkway. They walked over to the men and Lori asked politely, "Excuse me. We're looking for my mother. She's supposed to be in an art class up on this floor. Do you happen to know where the class is being held?" It soon became obvious that the men did not speak English. It appeared that their native language was Spanish. Julie and Lori were both enrolled in French classes at high school, which was no help to them in this situation. Somehow through the use of hand gestures and the few words of Spanish they knew (e.g., "ma madre" and "la classe"), they came to understand that the men were in Honolulu to participate in a boxing tournament and were staying at the "Y". One of them, Jose, was from Mexico and Manual was from El Salvador. They didn't know anything about an art class on the floor. The girls thanked them and headed back to the elevator which they took down to the lobby.

They soon located the front desk which was presided over by a matronly woman in her 50's. "Can you tell me where the art class is being held?" Lori asked the woman. "My mother told us to meet her there at noon". The woman frowned. "I don't know anything about an art class. Are you sure you're in the right place?" "Well", Lori replied, "she told me the class was on the third floor, but we were just up there and there was no sign of any classroom." The woman gasped, "I hope you weren't on the third floor – those are the men's dormitories – you're not supposed to be up there!" Lori blushed as she remembered the sight of the men's underwear hanging over the wall. "Well", she stammered, "All I know is she is taking an art class at the YWCA and we're supposed to meet her here." "Oh!" the woman exclaimed scornfully, "this is the YMCA. You want the YWCA. You need to go down to the next block and turn right. The YWCA is on the corner of Richards and Hotel Streets." Chagrinned the girls quickly took their leave of the matronly woman and exited the building. It was just 11:45 a.m. They still had time to get to the proper meeting place by noon.

Wood, Stain, And Electrical Outlets

Laurie Stoutz

I was built in 1923 by a prominent Eagle River Wisconsin builder, Louis Zimpleman. There have been many different family members who have enjoyed being sheltered by my walls, but there are two special caretakers I want to tell you about. My memory of the first one is "sketchy" because he was here 96 years ago. Scott Elijah Parsons was a Doctor, a general practitioner from St. Louis Missouri. He vacationed here with his family and friends. Eagle River is more pleasant than St Louis in the summer months, cool air without much humidity, blue skies, puffy white clouds and fragrant pine trees. Dr. Parsons and two other doctors came to the north woods of Wisconsin and purchased 100 feet of land from Edward Everett who owned the renowned Everett Resort. They all contracted with Mr. Zimpleman to build 3 cottages on their own share of the property, 33 feet each.

Let me tell you how much Scott Parson paid Mr Zimpleman to build me;

Complete House	$1967.53
Lot	$333.33
Furnishings	$610.40
Electric	$100.00
Build Road	$20.00
Insurance	$51.00
Incidentals	$19.26
TOTAL	$3,101.54

When I was built there was not a kitchen, nor a bathroom. The family took their main meals at the Everett Resort just up the road. I would hear the dinner bell ring and off they would go. In the beginning there were 3 bedrooms. In 1928 the Parsons decided to enclose the front porch making it into a sunroom and a bedroom. The cost of this conversion was $460.00, which included furnishings. Big changes came along in 1930. A kitchen and bath were added for $317.95 at the back of the house. (Please remember, the back is the roadside and the front is facing the lake). In 1931 the three doctors improved the property by putting in a joint water system, septic and a drywell. Dr. Parson's share was $282.00. Other changes happened in the early years. In 1925 the family purchased a boat for $135.00 and a Johnson motor for $135.00. In 1927 a second hand portable garage was bought for $100.00 and moved to the back of the property, it cost $89.00 to have it erected. Other interesting (quirky) facts about me, I have a wood box attached to my side; logs would be put in from the outside, and removed from inside for the wood burning stove. The Everett iceman would come and fill the icebox every day. There are not many changes that I remember between 1930 and 1950 but I was well taken care of by Dr Parsons and his family. More about how I am built, my bones, later.

Now I want to tell you about my early inhabitants. Along with Dr. Scott was his wife Mae, who unfortunately passed away in 1930. They had one daughter, Jane Frances Parsons. Jane loved coming here. One of her favorite pastimes was canoeing on Cranberry Lake in a green wooden canoe. It is still stored in my basement. Jane married Calvin Owen Stoutz Sr. in 1929. The next few years were not easy due to the Depression but Dr. Scott and his daughter Jane and Jane's 3 children spent summers here. Then in 1941 the family was not always able to come because of WWII. Jane and Calvin had three children, Jane, Calvin Jr. (Buddy) and Nancy. All of them loved being here in the north woods and continued to come and bring their own families. Some of the physical changes that occurred during this time were different heating systems; the inevitable fake wood paneling and updated electricity. Dr. Parsons lovingly cared for me until his passing in 1960.

Then his grandson took over, Calvin Jr. was a "diagnosis, fix-it kind" of man. He studied at Washington University in St Louis and graduated with a degree in Electrical Engineering. I can remember him crawling underneath me in the muddy leaves and in my attic so he could rewire the whole cottage. He loved putting in lots of light switches and electrical outlets. He also knew about plumbing and in 1999 moved the toilet to the opposite side of the bathroom so it was not visible from the dining room, a project his mother had wished for many years earlier.

Although Cal tried to take care of me he lived 1,000 miles away and only spent a couple of weeks with me each summer. During the 1970's and 80's Cal's mom, Cal and wife Barbara and their children Randy, Phil, Warren and Peg would vacation here. Cal's older sister Jane and her husband Dick Godlove and younger sister Nancy and her husband Don Hultquist would vacation with their families here too. I am not a spacious cottage but everyone especially Cal wanted to be here to take care of me.

Even though I looked sad and forgotten I did not feel abandoned. Sometimes strangers would come by and ask the neighbors why no one visited here, "was I for sale", they would ask. The neighbors would turn them away saying, "No the cottage is Not for Sale. There is a kind gentleman who comes every fall and does what he can to spruce it up."

In 1995 Cal brought his new wife Laurie for the first time. They enjoyed working together on projects and every year they set about to make me more presentable. They would dig in the sand and put in new cement pilings to help me stand straighter. Other projects included new tongue and groove ceiling in the kitchen, painting the garage, using old lumber from their other home to refresh my dining room walls, and scraping old linoleum and carpets off the floors.

In 2007 Cal and Laurie moved to Eagle River, making Wisconsin their home. Many changes came about in 2008. With the help of Bruce Kaitchuck and his team I was rolled on logs 75 feet forward towards the lake. A concrete slab was poured and basement walls were built and the cottage was rolled back onto the cement block walls and a new front and back porch were built. Then Calvin got to work. The words that best describe his projects are wood, stain and electric outlets. Let me repeat wood, stain and electric outlets. Almost every room was transformed with tongue and groove ceilings and wainscoting on the walls. Some people who update homes remove wood paneling, not Cal, he believed in keeping his beloved cottage in the tradition of the north woods, natural stained wood. A bedroom and an old porch were transformed into a beautiful kitchen overlooking Cranberry Lake. Cal ingeniously reused old kitchen cabinets to make an island and installed rails between the studs to make shelving for the dishes and glasses. An old storm window from a friend's home was added so that there is a wall of windows. Other projects included, crawling in the attic to rewire for fans and lighting fixtures and making all new screens for the bedroom windows. One of the messiest projects was jack hammering an old chimney out of the attic, carting the bricks through the hole in the bedroom ceiling and then outside. Cal's last projects included new railings on the porches and a new mailbox marking 1172 Cranberry Shores Road.

I am now owned by Cal's daughter Peggie and her husband Steve Bixler. Peg is the fourth generation of the Parson family to own me. I am sure the Bixlers will love me and care for me too, because this is their, "happy place". Some who read this might think it is just a list of construction projects but those who have known Cal will understand that it is a tribute to a very creative man who loved using his hands to refurbish a very special place with wood, stain and electrical outlets. Calvin Owen Stoutz passed away in 2019, I will miss his love, and care.

In loving memory of Calvin Owen Stoutz,
June 19,1932 – February 9, 2019

Since graduating from college, I have had a variety of positions; teaching in Pearl River NY, working at the Southeast YMCA in Pittsford NY, House Manager of the Rochester Ronald McDonald House, substitute teaching at Hammondsport Central School. I am now retired and live at the Villas of Canandaigua and love to travel to visit family and especially, spend time at Cal's beloved cottage.

Prime Time

Lisa Albrecht

Shelby gingerly brushed his fingers across the thin, transparent, blue paper. He loved the way his fingers slipped over its smooth surface, the way it made that crinkling sound as he clandestinely turned page over page in the back of the store. He pulled the large 18 x 24 tablet out from under the smaller ones. He had saved up enough money for the paper, plus a little extra – maybe some pens, or a new eraser might be nice. He walked over to the pen and pencil aisle. A forest of colored sticks stretched from wall to wall, one shade bleeding into the next. It was so alarmingly beautiful - the array of reds and oranges, blues and violets. Shelby walked to the end of the aisle, passing up on the succulent Caran Dache aquarelles and the creamy Holbein pastels. Nor was he seduced by the Stabilo markers, brush-tipped and dripping with bright urgency. He hurried by them, actually, looking past them, as if with one glance he would fall from the Garden. His destination was at the other end, among the monochromatic collection of blacks, whites, and a few cream-colored cylinders. Each concealed a gray graphite stick or a liquid shaft of blue or black ink. The drafting pens and mechanical pencils - all safely dull and muted, protected from any sudden outburst of color or heightened expression. He preferred that – it was much safer.

As he fondled his way through the pens, testing each nib on the small white pieces of scrap paper, the clerk watched him curiously from behind the counter. He recognized Shelby as a regular, of sorts. About every four to six months, Shelby made an appearance to buy more blueprint paper. The clerk had at first assumed that he was an errand boy for a small architectural firm, or even a novice draftsman, but he soon began to doubt his assumptions. Indeed, there was something odd about the way Shelby looked around the store, back over his shoulder, as he waded through the stacks – and he seldom made eye contact when he came to the counter to pay for his purchases.

He saw Shelby moving nervously toward the register.

"Did you find everything ok?"

Silence.

"Will that be all for you then, sir?"

"Y-yes, that's all", Shelby quietly replied, throwing his glance downward at the counter.

The clerk rang up the items.

"That's thirty-five dollars and eighty cents, unless you have a corporate discount account num-"

"No – no number", Shelby interrupted. He had been through this before.

Before I Forget

Shelby handed him a twenty, three fives and correct change. He almost always tried to pay with correct change. The clerk put the papers and pens in a large, brown paper bag. It was thin and smooth and made almost the same, familiar crinkly sound that the blueprint paper did - that soothing, crunchy sound.

He took the bag from the clerk and without saying thank you, walked through the door, letting it close behind him, the bell inside jingling as he walked away. The clerk watched him through the large glass storefront, as he passed between the "SALE" sign and the Rapidograph display.

"Odd ball", he muttered to himself.

Shelby normally walked home, but after glancing at his watch, he decided to take the bus. He wanted to have time to eat something before he began the next stage of his project at eight o'clock. And luckily, the bus was within view.

He boarded and dropped his fare into the meter. The bus lumbered uptown, each cross street peeling away a different part of the city. After a few blocks they passed through a large intersection which, looking west, provided a full view of the new Public Library – a vast, orange cube of a building, the most modern of all the downtown structures. It was where Shelby worked. He had worked in the library system for almost ten years, moving into Biographies and Performing Arts when the new branch opened. This line of work was not disagreeable to him – the hours were normal; the work was easy enough and still somewhat intellectually stimulating. He rather liked collecting the sundry bits of information that settled in his head, just from having a few hundred books pass through his hands every day. It was exponential. He liked to think that it was all remembered somewhere, in his brain.

Shelby arrived home to his one-bedroom duplex in about fifteen minutes. Entering through the side door, he flicked on the light and tossed his keys on the table. He put the paper bag in the living room and proceeded to nuke a Hungry Man TV Dinner: turkey with peas and carrots, stuffing, mashed potatoes with butter, and apple-cranberry compote. It was his favorite meal ritual every week, prior to project time. Quick and delicious, he always took it out of the freezer to thaw before leaving for work in the morning, even though he knew he didn't have to. He just wanted to be sure.

He always dined on the coffee table in the living room, switching on the TV with the remote. Only a few more minutes to go! He sorted through the stuffing, pushing the drier, uncooked croutons to the side, holding out for the moister bits hidden under the meat. Loud voiceovers filled the room, the alternating intensity of the television screen flashed across his torso. He ate voraciously.

As the commercials and news breaks continued to issue forth, Shelby reached back over the end of the couch and into his backpack, pulling out a long, white tube and opened the end. He removed a blue print from inside. He put the TV dinner tray on the floor and spread the print open, securing the corners with an amber paperweight and three small beach stones he had collected on a trip to the Gulf when he was ten. Then he produced a slide ruler, T square, and a mechanical pencil - the Berol TC-9- his personal favorite. He was ready.

Then the familiar theme song began: "Tell me why...I love you like I do, tell me who...." A faint smile rested on the corners of his otherwise straight lips. The much-anticipated episode of *Mad About You* was underway at last! Shelby's heart was filled with the familiar warmth of seeing a long-lost friend. He was utterly delighted. This was his safe haven.

He suddenly sprang from the couch. "DAMMIT!" Lunging toward the set, he pulled a video tape from the shelf and shoved it into the VCR. "REC" appeared in the lower left corner of the screen. He breathed a deep sigh of relief, having only missed a few seconds of the opening credits.

This week he was working on Paul and Jaime's apartment. He had already completed a full set of Seinfeld blueprints: Jerry's apartment - the diner - Kramer's place - Elaine's office - George's parent's apartment. These were painstakingly preserved and kept in his bedroom. He would open them from time to time to add more details, or simply to gaze proudly at them, admiring the good work he had done. There were bundles of others that he finished, all from the mid-80's. But his most prized set was without question, the complete set of the apartments and houses that the Ricardos and Mertzes had lived in during six seasons of *I Love Lucy*. Thanks to the ubiquitous reruns and *Nick at Nite*, he was able to render those drawings with incredible accuracy. Once, when he visited the Smithsonian while on a class trip, he was able to view the exhibit of the actual set from the old series – there it was, the Ricardo's living room, all laid out with the original sofa and chairs, end tables and mantelpiece. Shelby was beside himself with delight, as the accuracy of his own blueprints was confirmed. His other vintage prints included the *Dick Van Dyck Show* and of course, *The Andy Griffith Show*. But truth be told, he was actually quite satisfied with his most recent work on *Mad About You*. He thought it was some of his best.

Now he turned his attention to the action, his eyes becoming glued to the screen. He studied each shot carefully, jotting down notes, sometimes on a pad, sometimes on the blueprint itself. One would have thought he was trying to memorize a script. But Shelby wasn't interested in plot, character, or comedy writing. He was studying the rooms – the layout, the floor plan – in which the characters moved. He was carefully denoting each angle, approximating depth, width, length, square footage and furniture positions. He was scrupulous about the details, leaving nothing unnoticed. And after each weekly episode, he would assimilate these findings, these details, onto his blueprint.

Shelby had begun this fascination, this obsession in the 70's. All in the Family was about the only thing that ever brought him, his parents and his older sister together, in one place, at one time. It was their Saturday night vigil. He started out on graph paper then eventually moved on to larger sheets of newsprint that he had found in the school art room closet, which he absconded with after hours. He would work late at night after everyone else had gone to bed. Once, during one of the all too frequent drunken binges, his father discovered him bent over his desk, working on the layout of Archie and Edith's living room. He stumbled over to Shelby, grabbed him by the nape of the neck and slurred a strain of derogatory words at him, telling him to get the hell to bed and that he didn't want to see him drawing any more stupid, faggot pictures anymore, or else. Shelby cowered in the corner until his father left. His father liked to belittle him about it – about most everything. Shelby rolled up his papers and hid them for weeks, until he felt it might be safe again.

Even now, it was the center of his life – what he lived for. He had honed his skills through a Basic Draftsmanship book that he found in the discard bin at the library and had graduated to blueprint paper about two years ago, to give it a more professional look. Capturing the details of the lives of those people in their perfect TV world, their friends, families, the places where their good times happened, where people could come together for twenty-two minutes of laughter, conflict, and then laughter again, made him feel close to them, to something he lacked. It was like he had a special family of his own.

Now he concentrated hard on the entryway to the Kitchen. Paul and Jaime had just argued about who would return their friend's wedding gift; Murray the dog paced tiresomely in front of the couch. Shelby added a few more feet between the doorway and the bookcase. He knew they would work out their problems. He smiled as he erased a line and redrew it to a more perfect scale, while Paul and Jaime kissed and made up in the foreground. Jaime was so beautiful, he thought, her blond hair falling delicately over her shoulders as Paul held her close. Once again, everything had turned out just right.

The Cupboard

Amy K. Herlehy

Warm does not begin to describe the day. Oppressive, with a little sprinkle of excitement and perspiration are more like it. Mom, my sister and I were headed to the Madison Bouckville Antique market. It was 6:00 AM and with water bottles, hats and carts in tow we set out for an adventure. Over 2,000 dealers pedaling their wares. We all had delusions of grandeur that we would find the perfect item for our homes. The anticipation of finding a sleeper loomed large and it was every woman for herself, even among relatives. It was a smorgasbord of everything old, odd and original and we were drooling at the opportunity to participate.

Picture a cow pasture with greasy food vendors, porta -potties and golf carts and you pretty much get the picture. Add to that the steamy heat and well, you get the idea. I had partaken in this venue before but mom and my sister were new to this field of Dreams. They were used to me moving quickly down the aisles in fear I might miss something. They strolled behind me taking careful inspection of items while I continued my march on. My sister reveled at only the finest antiques while my mom looked for the best buys and I was all about primitive painted antiques. We all had very different styles and tastes but the passion for what we were doing was clear. None of us needed anything but whoever does? It is all about want. It was a bond that tied us together. It made us feel supported, close and everything else in the world at that very moment didn't exist. Though don't get me wrong we were still highly competitive with our finds. If two of us spotted an item at the same time we had to have a discussion around who saw it first and whose house it would go in. This usually took place between my mom and I because my sister was out of our price range with her purchases. Mom usually relented because she was always putting others ahead of herself.

A quick break to consume a hot dog and lemonade would give us enough energy to keep on going. We finished the majority of all 2,000 booths and were rounding the corner to end our journey with dirt stained legs and faces and there it was. The mother of all cupboards. It was big and it had old crusty red paint on it. My adrenaline started to kick in and I could feel my energy rise but I had to play it cool. What was the price of this beauty? (My husband, brother in law and father would beg to differ) Was there anyone else looking at it? How eager was the dealer to sell it? I had to have it. It would be perfect for our family room as a TV cabinet. After I used my stellar negotiating skills the cupboard was mine. My mom and sister were laughing because they knew I wouldn't make it out of there without buying something big.

There was one small detail I overlooked. Would it fit in the car? At the time we had my mom's Volvo wagon. No problem it would be fine or would it? We pulled the car up and jammed that big red cupboard in the back of the Volvo. It fit perfect. It took every ounce of cargo area in that car. Oops where are we going to sit. Mom driving, me in the passenger sit and thank goodness my sister is skinny. She climbed on top of that big red cupboard on her stomach and rode the whole way home (2 ½ hours) without a single complaint. After we got home, she told my mom, "Amy has dragged a lot of stuff around for me and I wasn't going to let her down".

Our bond, our memories our story.

CPSIA information can be obtained
at www.ICGtesting.com
Printed in the USA
BVHW030302081119
563268BV00001B/34/P